4

j398   Mabinogion
M112t   Tales from The Mabinogion, retold by
            Olwen Bowen.   Illus. by Richard Kennedy.
            N.Y., Vanguard, c1969.
                              5.95   78-155665

4-76   1.Wales--Folklore. I.Title.

TALES FROM THE MABINOGION

Tales from the Mabinogion

retold by OLWEN BOWEN

ILLUSTRATED BY RICHARD KENNEDY

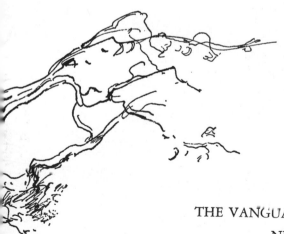

THE VANGUARD PRESS, INC.

NEW YORK, N.Y.

For
ESSYLLT

Acknowledgement

My grateful thanks are due to
Mr Caradoc Pritchard, who has
helped me with matters of
pronunciation and derivation.

O. B.

Contents

TALES OF PRINCE PWYLL

Pwyll Prince of Dyved

LONG ago, before history was written and when there were no books in which to read of the doings of our ancestors, these stories were told by the Bards, who sang of the kings and princes and great men of the island.

In these far away days in South Wales there was a prince called Pwyll, who ruled over the country of Dyved, and the Bards sang of his doings. They told how, one morning, when he was living at his chief palace at Narberth, he went out hunting. All day he hunted and rested at night, and at dawn the next day he set out to follow his hounds, riding at such a speed that he left his huntsmen behind. And as he was listening to his hounds, who were hot on the scent, he heard the baying of other hounds that were not of his pack and seemed to come from the opposite direction.

Following quickly, he saw his hounds come to an open glade in the wood, and in this glade was a stag beset by strange hounds, unlike any that he had ever seen before. Their hair was shining white, while their ears glistened with a bright red. Then Prince Pwyll drove off the strange pack and set his own hounds on the stag.

At that moment a man in grey woollen hunting clothes with a hunting-horn slung round his neck rode towards him on a large, light grey horse and called out to him:

"Chieftain, I know who you are, but I give you no greeting."

Prince Pwyll asked why this should be. Was the huntsman of too noble birth to be willing to talk to him?

"It is not my dignity which stops me," answered the huntsman, "but your ignorance and want of courtesy, that you should drive off my hounds which had brought down the stag and set your own upon him."

"Oh Chieftain," cried Prince Pwyll, "I have done you wrong! I should like to apologize and atone for my ill deed so that we may be friends."

"And how will you atone?" asked the huntsman.

"How can I tell what you would wish me to do," replied Prince Pwyll, "when I do not know who you are?"

"A crowned king am I," answered the huntsman. "Arawn is my name, and I am King of Annwyvn."

"And will you tell me how I may gain your friendship, oh King?"

"I will tell you," said Arawn. "There is a king called Havgan, whose kingdom lies opposite to mine and who is forever waging war on my people. If you will rid me of this tyrant, which you could easily do, then you shall indeed gain my friendship."

"I will gladly help you," answered Prince Pwyll, "if you will tell me what I must do."

Then Arawn said that it was within his power to transform Pwyll into an exact likeness of himself, so that nobody should know the difference. "And then you must be King of Annwyvn in my place and rule my country for one year from tomorrow. I will give you as companion the most beautiful lady you have ever seen, and no one of my servants and subjects shall know that you are not me."

"But what shall I do about my own kingdom?" asked the Prince. "Who will govern while I am away?"

"I will take on your likeness," answered Arawn, "and I will rule in your place for the year that you are away, and none shall know of the change."

"And how am I to find your enemy?"

"It is arranged that a year from tonight he and I are to meet at the Ford. You shall be there in my place and shall give him one stroke, which shall kill him. And if he begs you to strike him again, you must not do so, for this is what happened to me when I met him before. My first blow struck him down; but at my second he recovered and fought with me the next day as strongly as ever."

"I will gladly do this for you," said Prince Pwyll. So Arawn led him away and showed him the kingdom which he was to rule for a year, and Prince Pwyll found that he was so much like Arawn that nobody on looking at them could see any difference.

So he parted from Arawn and went on until he came to the Palace of his new kingdom, and he found that it was the most beautiful that he had ever seen, his dress was of the richest, and he was waited on better than he had ever been in his life. When he went in to dine the Queen sat beside him, and he thought that she was the most beautiful and the noblest lady that he had ever met.

Prince Pwyll lived for a year in this country in the greatest luxury, spending his leisure time hunting and feasting and listening to the minstrels, until a year had passed and the time came for him to meet Arawn's enemy at the Ford, and he set out, attended by the nobles of the Court.

When he reached the Ford, Havgan and his warriors were there to meet him. Then, from among the nobles who had come with Prince Pwyll, one stepped forward and addressed the assembled crowds.

"My lords," he cried, "this is a meeting of two great kings. Each king claims a right to the other's lands, and the dispute is between them and them only. Therefore let us all stand aside, and let these two great kings settle the matter by personal combat."

Then the two kings stepped forward into the water, each from his own side, and met in the middle of the Ford. Remembering his instructions, Prince Pwyll, whom all took to be Arawn, gave Havgan a mighty blow which split his shield in two and, crashing through his armour, brought him to the ground. Then Havgan,

knowing the blow to be fatal, cried out: "What right have you to kill me? I have done you no harm. But as you have given me my death-blow I beg you in the name of Heaven to finish quickly the work you have begun."

Then Pwyll, remembering the warning of Arawn, said: "Not so, my lord! Kill you who may, I will not do it lest I may be sorry for what I have done."

And Havgan called to his followers to carry him away, for the time of his death had come, "And I can no longer protect you."

At this Prince Pwyll, still speaking as Arawn, called out to the warriors who had come with Havgan and were gathered on the far side of the Ford:

"My lords and friends, who would you now have for your rightful ruler?" and they answered him:

"Lord, there is but one king now over the whole of Annwyvn, and we are all your subjects." And Prince Pwyll then received the homage of the nobles, and by the next day the two kingdoms were united in his power.

After that Prince Pwyll went to keep his promise and meet the real Arawn as they had arranged, and great was the rejoicing of the two kings when they saw each other again.

"May Heaven reward you for your friendship," said Arawn, "for I have heard of all the good you have done both for my kingdom and for me. And when you get back to your own land you will see that I in my turn have worked for you, and I hope you will feel that I have repaid you properly."

"Whatever you have done for me," said Prince Pwyll of Dyved, "may Heaven repay you."

Then Arawn restored Pwyll to his own shape and likeness, and again took upon himself the form of Arawn, and, bidding Prince Pwyll a courteous farewell, he returned to his kingdom of Annwyvn. He was glad to see his home again and to be once more among his own people.

Prince Pwyll also returned to his rightful country and, calling his courtiers together, he asked for their opinion of how he had governed for the last year.

"Lord," they said, "never have you ruled so well, and never has your wisdom been so great."

"Then give your thanks to the man who has earned them," answered Pwyll, and told the whole story to his nobles. Great was their astonishment, and they begged Pwyll that he would not let them be cut off from the wisdom of the man who had given them the wise government they had enjoyed for the past year.

"I promise you that it shall be as you wish," said Prince Pwyll. "There shall be a lasting alliance between the two countries, and we shall still benefit by the wisdom of this great king." Thus a strong friendship grew up between the two rulers, who sent presents of horses, greyhounds, hawks and jewels to each other, and the two countries lived in the closest amity from that time onwards.

Prince Pwyll's Bride

ONE day Prince Pwyll held a feast at Narberth, his chief palace, and after the meat had been served he left the table and went for a walk, taking a path which led to the top of a mound behind the palace.

Then a member of his Court called out to him: "Lord, do you know the truth about that mound? It is said that whoever sits on it cannot leave it until he has either received wounds and blows or has seen a wonder."

"I am not afraid of wounds and blows while I am in the midst of my own people," said Pwyll, "and I should be glad to see a wonder," and he went on up the mound and sat down on the top of it.

While he was sitting there he saw a lady riding on a large horse of pure white coming slowly towards him at an even pace, and her dress was of pure gold. Then the Prince called out to his men to ask who the lady might be; but none of them knew.

"Send to meet her," he ordered, "that we may find out who she is!"

At once a nobleman went out to greet the stranger; but she took no notice of him and rode on past, and he, being on foot, was unable to overtake the great white horse. When he realized that he would never be able to catch up with the lady, he hurried back to the mound and told the Prince what had happened.

"Go quickly back to the Palace!" commanded the Prince. "Take the fastest horse in the stables and ride after her!"

So the nobleman hurriedly found a horse and, spurring it forward over the level plain, went after the lady. But the faster he rode the greater grew the distance between them, though she appeared to be moving no quicker than she had before. At last the pace became too great for the nobleman's horse, which began to tire and could no longer go forward; so he turned round and made his way back to the mound on which Prince Pwyll sat.

"My lord Prince," he said, "this is the fastest horse I know of, but even he could not overtake the lady."

"There is something strange here," answered Pwyll. "Let us return to the Palace, and tomorrow I will go to the mound again at the same time." Then he turned to one of his young courtiers. "And you will come with me," he said, "on the swiftest horse that you can find."

This they did, and once more the lady was seen riding towards the mound. As she drew near to them Pwyll told the youth to ride forward and speak to her so that they might learn the name of their beautiful visitor.

As the young courtier hurried to mount his horse she drew level with them and passed by the mound, and he quickly rode after her. But though he was only a little way behind the great white horse, and though its pace appeared no faster than it had been the day before, he was unable to draw level with her. So he increased his pace; but even when his horse was galloping at its fastest and the lady seemed to be moving at a leisurely pace, still he could not come any nearer to her. So he returned to Prince Pwyll, who had been watching.

"I see," said the Prince, "that it is useless to try to follow the lady. She must indeed be on some very important errand if she cannot spare the time to pause for a moment to give us a greeting. Let us return to the Palace and continue our feast."

On the third day of the feast Prince Pwyll called to his nobles once more to accompany him to the mound, and commanded that his own horse should be saddled and taken down to the road to be ready for him to ride, and once more he went and sat on the mound. Again the lady appeared riding towards them, and at once Prince Pwyll mounted his horse. As he did so the lady passed by, and he rode forward, expecting that only a few paces would bring him level with her. But as he went forward she had ridden ahead of him, and though he spurred his horse on to its greatest speed he could not overtake her.

So the Prince called out in a loud voice: "Oh maiden, for the sake of him whom you love best, wait for me!"

"I will gladly stay," said the maiden, "and it would have been better for your horse if you had spoken sooner." Then she stopped and waited for him and, throwing back her veil, she looked full into his face and talked with him.

"Lady," he cried, "where do you come from and whither do you travel?"

"I travel on my own errands," she answered, "and I am indeed glad to see you."

Then Prince Pwyll gave her welcome; and of all the fair ladies he had ever seen he found her the most beautiful.

"Will you tell me what your errand is?" he asked.

"I came to seek for you," she answered.

This gave Pwyll great joy, and he begged her to tell him who she was.

"I am Rhiannon the daughter of Heveydd Hên," she answered. "They tried to force me to marry against my will; but I will take no husband because of my love for you, and unless you reject me I will marry no one else."

"Lady," said Prince Pwyll, "if I might choose between all the maidens of the world, you would be my choice for a wife."

"If that is really so," replied Rhiannon, "you must act quickly before I am given to another."

"The sooner we are married the better for my happiness," declared Pwyll. "Tell me what I must do!"

"You shall come to Heveydd's palace twelve months from today," said Rhiannon, "and I will have a feast prepared for your welcome."

"Gladly will I come," answered Pwyll, and the lady, after once more telling him how important it was that he should keep his promise, rode off and was soon out of sight.

Then Prince Pwyll went back to his courtiers; but when they asked him what had happened and what he and the lady had talked about, he would tell them nothing.

When at last the year had passed and the time had come for the Prince to claim his bride, he took with him a hundred knights and rode in state to the palace of Heveydd Hên. There he was welcomed with great rejoicings, and the whole Court was placed at his disposal, and there was much revelry and feasting.

While they feasted, as Prince Pwyll sat at table by the side of his future bride, a tall youth with auburn hair and royal bearing came before them, and Prince Pwyll greeted him and asked him to be seated.

"I will not," declared the youth, "for I have come to ask a boon."

"Whatever you ask it shall be given to you," said the Prince; but Rhiannon cried out that he should not have given a promise before before he knew what was asked.

"He has given his promise," answered the young man, "before all the nobles of this court, and I claim my boon. It is that I should have for my bride the beautiful Rhiannon, the lady I love best. I come to ask you for her, together with this banquet, which shall be the feast for me and my bride."

Then Pwyll was filled with sorrow and said nothing at all.

"Be silent as long as you will," cried Rhiannon, "for never did man speak so foolishly as you did when you promised him that he should have whatever he asked; for this is Gwawl, the man to whom they tried to marry me against my will. And now you must give me to him because of your promise, for he is a very powerful man, and if you break your word you will be greatly shamed."

"Never will I allow this," said Prince Pwyll.

"You must," answered Rhiannon. "Give me to him, and I will see to it that I am never his."

Then she told Pwyll that she would give him a small, magic bag which he must keep carefully. "And he will demand that you give him this banquet also, which you cannot do for it is not yours to give. And I will tell him that a year from this night he shall have a feast of his own, and then I will be his bride. And when we are at this feast you must come in, dressed in rags and carrying this bag. And when it happens that you are offered a boon you must ask nothing but that the bag be filled with food. This Gwawl will promise you, and you will find that however much food and drink is put into the bag there will always be room for more. They will then ask you if your bag will never be full, and you must answer that it never will until a nobleman of great wealth will come and press the food into the bag with both his feet, saying as he does so: 'Enough has been put therein.' I will then make Gwawl come forward himself and tread down your food, and when he does this you must turn the bag so that he is in it right up to his head. Then, quickly, you must pull up the string of the bag and tie a knot in it."

She also told Pwyll that he must wear a bugle round his neck, and as soon as he has tied the knot he must blow a call upon his bugle as a signal to his warriors to come from the orchard into the palace.

So the banquet ended. Gwawl said goodbye to the beautiful Rhiannon and declared that he would return a year from that day to claim her as his bride, while Pwyll returned sorrowfully to his own country, carrying with him the magic bag.

On the same day a year later Prince Pwyll went once more to the palace of Heveydd Hên, again attended by a hundred noblemen. This time he bade them hide in the orchard until summoned by his bugle, when they were to come in a body to the palace. Then he dressed himself in rags and, wearing clumsy old shoes, went on alone towards the palace. He arrived in the middle of the feast and bowed low before Gwawl, who now sat in the seat of honour beside the Princess. Gwawl greeted him kindly and said: "If you ask anything of me that is just, then I will give it to you."

"I am poor and needy," answered Pwyll. "All I ask is to have this little bag filled with food."

"Gladly will I grant this boon," answered Gwawl.

Then the servants brought food which they put into the bag, and more food and more again; but still there was room for more in the bag.

"Will your bag never be full?" asked Gwawl at last.

"Never," answered Prince Pwyll, "until a man who owns much land and great riches shall tread down the food that is in the bag with both his feet."

Then Rhiannon turned to Gwawl and told him to go quickly and tread down the food for fear that all their provisions might be taken, and Gwawl left the table and did as she said. Then Pwyll drew up the bag over Gwawl's head, fastened it with a firm knot and blew a loud call on his bugle.

At once his nobles rushed in from the orchard, overcame Gwawl's attendants, and threw them into the palace prisons, and each of Prince Pwyll's followers as he came in hit the bag and asked: "What is in the bag?"

"A badger!" was the answer, and they struck it again, crying out: "This is the game of Badger in the Bag."

"Lord Prince," cried a voice from the bag, "surely I do not deserve to be killed in a bag!"

"That is true," said King Heveydd Hên, and, turning to Prince Pwyll, he went on: "You should have mercy on him, for he does not deserve this fate."

Then Rhiannon suggested that if Gwawl were let out of the bag he should pay the minstrels and all that had come to the feast to ask for help, and also that he must undertake never to seek revenge for what had been done to him.

"Willingly will I promise this," cried Gwawl, and King

Heveydd Hên said that he would vouch for his good faith, and he was set free. Then, being badly bruised and in need of help, Gwawl asked if he might go, leaving behind him certain of his nobles as a pledge of his honesty and his will to fulfil his promise.

Then Prince Pwyll removed his rags and took his place at the feast, claiming Rhiannon as his bride, and all went on as though it were the feast of the year before, and great were the rejoicings at the palace. And the next day Prince Pwyll and Rhiannon his bride set off together for the country of Dyved.

Prince Pwyll's Son

FOR three years Prince Pwyll and his beautiful wife lived happily together in the palace of Narberth; but they had no children, and there was much sorrow and discontent in the country because there was no heir to the throne. And the nobles sent to the Prince to ask him if he would not take another wife, as then he might perhaps have a son.

"We have only been married three years," said the Prince. "Leave us one more year, and if we have no son by then I will do as you say."

So the nobles ceased to bother him. The royal couple were left in peace, and by the end of the year a son was born to Rhiannon. Great were the rejoicings in the country, and for fear that any ill should befall the babe six women were placed to watch through the night in the room in which he and his mother slept.

But one by one the women fell asleep, and by midnight there was no one awake to guard the young prince. When at last the women woke they found to their horror that the child had vanished.

"What can we do?" they cried. "We were put here to watch him, and he is lost. We shall have some terrible punishment and will probably be put to death," and they were all very much afraid.

Then one of the women had an idea. "The Queen has a staghound," she said, "that has a litter of puppies. Let us kill some of these and rub the blood on the Queen's face and hands, and spread the bones of the puppies before her. We can then say that Rhiannon herself has killed her baby son and eaten him. And when she says that it is not so, we shall be six against one, and so we shall be believed and no harm will come to us."

And so it was agreed.

When morning came Rhiannon woke up and asked where her son was.

"Lady," said the women, "here we are, covered with bruises from the blows you gave us when we tried to rescue the baby from you, and now *you* ask *us* where your son is! We have never seen anyone so violent as you were in the night when you fought us back and devoured the baby before our eyes."

The good Queen was overcome with horror at the tale they told.

"For pity's sake do not make false accusations against me!" she cried. "If you are afraid because he has gone and you were there to guard him, then I vow that I will protect you and no harm shall come to you, only tell me the truth, I beg of you."

But the women were too much afraid, and they refused to tell anything but the lie they had made up.

The story spread quickly through the palace, and soon it was known all over the country. The nobles came to Prince Pwyll in great indignation and demanded that he should put away his wife because of the dreadful thing she had done.

But the Prince answered that they had no right to expect him to put her away. "She is my wife," he said, "and I shall certainly stand by her. But if she has done wrong let her do penance for it."

Try as she would, Rhiannon could not make the six women admit that their story was not true; so she sent for the wise men of the country and asked them to decide what penance she must do.

After consulting among themselves the wise men told her that the penance they demanded of her was that she should stay in the palace of Narberth for seven years, and that every day of those seven years she should sit beside a mounting-block which was just outside the gates. And she must stop all the people who came to the palace and tell them the story of her crime if they did not know it already, and that she should ask the visitors if they would allow her to carry them on her back up to the door of the palace.

This penance Rhiannon agreed to, and she went at once to take her place outside the gate, and this she did daily, and so passed many months.

Now it so happened that there lived in South Wales a great and noble man called Teirnyon, who owned the most beautiful mare in the kingdom. Each year, on the night of the first of May, a foal was born to the mare, yet not one of her young colts had ever been seen by any man. Now again the first of May was approaching, and Teirnyon, expecting the mare to produce another foal, was determined to find out what it was that each year stole away the colts. So he ordered that the mare should be brought into the house, armed himself and prepared to watch through the night.

As he had expected, a foal was born in the night, and as he was admiring its beauty and its size he heard a loud commotion outside the window. Before he had time to find out the cause of the noise a great claw thrust in through the window and seized the colt by its mane. Then Teirnyon drew his sword and cut off the arm at the elbow, and so saved the colt from being drawn up and out of the window.

The noise outside grew louder, and there was a great wailing. Waiting not a moment, Teirnyon rushed out; but the night was dark and he could not see what was there. He was hurrying away after the wailing sound when he remembered that he had come out in such a rush that he had forgotten to shut the door, and fearing for the colt, he turned and ran back to the house. At the open door he found a baby boy wrapped in a satin mantle. He picked up the child, and was surprised at the strength in so small a baby. He took the boy at once to his sleeping wife and, waking her up, said: "My lady, here is a baby boy which you can keep if you would like to," and he told her all that had happened. Together they looked at the child and at the fine clothes in which he was wrapped, which made them believe that he had come of a noble family.

"I will keep him," she said, "and I will pretend that he is really our own."

So Teirnyon and his wife had the boy baptized and brought him up as if he were indeed their own son, and he grew in beauty and strength, and his hair was as yellow as gold. Before he was a year old not only could he walk well, but he was larger than an ordinary child of three would be: and at the end of his second year he was as large as a child of six. He grew so fast in mind and body that before he was five he would bribe the grooms to let him take the horses to the water.

One day Teirnyon's wife asked her husband what had become of the colt which he had rescued on the night that the baby was found.

"I have told the grooms that they must take great care of him," he answered.

"Would it not be a good idea," said his lady, "if you were to have the colt broken in and give it to the boy, as the rescue of the one was on the same night as the finding of the other?"

Teirnyon agreed to this, and his wife was so pleased that she went at once to the grooms and ordered that the horse should be broken in by the time the boy was old enough to ride him.

It was not until now that the rumour of Rhiannon's supposed crime and her punishment reached the home of Teirnyon and his wife. The story troubled them, and they did not rest till they had found out all the details, for they were filled with pity that such a terrible sorrow had come to the beautiful and honoured lady. Teirnyon thought deeply of all that had happened and, gazing at his adopted son, saw in him a great likeness to Pwyll, Prince of Dyved, whom he knew well, having once been one of his followers. Then he thought to himself: "This is unmistakably the likeness of a son to his father. What right have I to keep him with me now that I know him to be the son of another man, and

to allow so great a punishment to fall on so excellent and innocent a lady as Rhiannon?"

He talked it over with his wife, and they agreed that the boy must be sent to Pwyll, who was undoubtedly his rightful father.

"And the sacrifice of giving up the boy will also do us good," declared the lady, "for we shall gain in three ways. We shall be given thanks and gifts for relieving Rhiannon of her punishment, thanks from Pwyll for looking after his son and restoring him to his father, and thirdly the boy himself will, out of gratitude, do us all the good he can."

The next day Teirnyon, taking with him two knights, rode towards Narberth with the boy, who was mounted on the horse which his adopted father had given him. And as they came up to the palace gate they saw Rhiannon sitting beside the horse-block.

"Chieftain," she cried, "go no further, for I will carry you and your three companions on my back up to the Palace. This is my penance for killing my own son and eating him."

"Oh fair lady," answered Teirnyon, "I will never allow you to do such a thing!"

"Neither will I," cried the boy, and they went on up to the palace, where they found that a feast was being prepared to welcome Prince Pwyll home from his travels.

Pwyll made Teirnyon welcome and placed him in the seat of honour at the feast, between himself and Rhiannon. After the meat had been served and eaten they began talking, and Teirnyon told of his adventures with the mare and the finding of the boy, and how he and his wife had brought the child up as their son. Then, turning to Rhiannon, he said:

"Lady, behold, for here is your son, and whoever told the tale of your crime has spoken wicked lies. When I heard the story I was very grieved, for there can be none who look at the boy who will doubt from his likeness to his father that he is Prince Pwyll's son," and all the courtiers agreed that the likeness was strong enough to leave no doubt in the matter.

"If this is true," cried Rhiannon, "then it is the end of my troubles and my anxiety."

And they decided then and there that the boy's name should be Pryderi, which means Anxiety, because that was the word his mother used when she heard the joyful news.

Then Prince Pwyll poured out thanks to Teirnyon for all that he had done for the child, and he added: "As the boy is of princely blood it is right that he should repay you for your care of him."

"My lord," replied Teirnyon, "it is my wife who had the work of bringing up the child, and she is very sorrowful at parting with him. Let him not forget us and what we have done for him."

"I swear to you," said Pwyll, "that for so long as I live I will be indebted to you and will look after you and your possessions to the best of my ability. And when the boy comes into power he will do the same, even better than I can. And I will have the boy brought up by Pendaran Dyved, who is a near neighbour of yours, so that you shall still be companions, and he shall look upon you both as his foster fathers."

Then he offered Teirnyon gifts of the fairest jewels and the finest horses and the choicest dogs; but Teirnyon would take none of them, but parted from Prince Pwyll in great friendship and with much rejoicing, and journeyed back to his own home.

And Pryderi grew up as a young prince should, and became the handsomest youth in the country and the most skilled in all the good games, and so passed many years until the death of Prince Pwyll. Then Pryderi ruled in his father's stead, and added much land to the kingdom, which he governed well and wisely.

TALES OF THE CHILDREN OF LLYR,
KING OF THE ISLAND OF THE MIGHTY

Branwen the Daughter of Llyr

BENDIGEID Vran, the son of Llyr, sat one day upon the Rock of Harlech gazing out to sea. So great was he that no house could hold him, and he was King of all Britain. With him were many courtiers, his brother Manawyddan and his two half-brothers, Nissyen, a noble youth who loved peace and the happiness of his brothers, and Evnissyen, who was of a different nature and would cause enmity between his brothers when they had no thought of anything but friendship and peace.

As they watched they saw thirteen ships coming from the direction of southern Ireland. The wind was behind the ships, filling their sails, and they cut rapidly through the water towards the land. On seeing this the King commanded that his companions should send down men to the shore to find out to whom the ships belonged and their object in coming to Britain. So a band of courtiers went down to the beach, and later, when reporting to the King, they told him that they had never seen ships better equipped. Beautiful satin flags flew from them, and as one of the ships drew ahead of the others a shield was lifted above the side, its point turned upwards in token of peace. Boats were then lowered and rowed towards the land, and the sailors cried salutes to the King of Britain.

So near were they that Bendigeid Vran could hear what they said from where he sat on the rock, and he called out to welcome them.

"To whom do these ships belong?" he asked. "And who is the chief among you?"

"Lord," they cried, "Matholwch, King of Ireland, is here, and these ships belong to him."

Bendigeid Vran then asked why the King had come, and courteously invited him to land.

"He comes to ask a boon of thee," the messenger replied, "and unless he may have it he will not land. He wishes to ally himself with you, and begs that he may marry your sister, Branwen the daughter of Llyr, that Britain and Ireland may be united in friendship and thus both become more powerful."

"Ask him to come ashore," said Bendigeid Vran, "and we will talk the matter over and take advice of our counsellors."

So Matholwch came to land and was greeted royally, and that night Bendigeid Vran entertained him and his followers, and great was the rejoicing.

The next day Bendigeid Vran took advice of his counsellors and agreed to bestow the hand of his sister, the beautiful Branwen, upon Matholwch. It was decided that the wedding should take place at Aberffraw, and Bendigeid Vran and his Court set out by land, while Matholwch took his ships round to meet him there. Great was the crowd of courtiers and guests, and as no house could hold them, tents were put up in which the wedding-feast could be held, and Matholwch was married to the beautiful Branwen.

The following day Matholwch ordered that his troops should be arrayed, and to be ready for this his horses were brought from the ships and ranged in a line so long that it stretched from the tents to the sea. It so happened that Evnissyen, passing that way, saw the horses and asked to whom they belonged. When he heard that they were King Matholwch's, who was now Branwen's husband, he was very angry.

"Is this what has happened?" he said. "They have married my sister to this man without my consent? Never have I been so insulted," and he rushed at the horses with his sword and attacked them, harming them so that they could never be of use again.

When Matholwch heard of this he could hardly believe what his followers told him. "I do not understand it," he said. "Why, if the people of this country wished to insult me, did they give me their princess in marriage?"

"But nevertheless this is what they have done," cried his counsellors, "and there is nothing left for you but to leave the land."

So sadly Matholwch went down to the shore, embarked in his ships and sailed away from Britain.

When Bendigeid Vran heard that his guest had left so suddenly and without taking leave of himself and his Court he was much disturbed, and he sent messengers after Matholwch to ask why he had gone. The messengers soon caught up with the ships and were taken before Matholwch.

"If I had known what would happen I would never have come here," said Matholwch. "No one was ever so insulted as I have been. But this I do not understand: why, if your King intended to treat me in this way, did he agree to my marriage with his beautiful sister, the daughter of Llyr the King of the Island of the Mighty, and one of the three chief ladies in the land. If he wished to insult me he should surely have done so before the marriage took place."

"My lord," said the messengers, "all that has happened was without the knowledge of our King. That you, his honoured guest, should have received such treatment in his country, is a greater insult to him than it is to you."

"I agree," said Matholwch. "Nevertheless the insult has been given, and nothing he can do will take it away."

When Bendigeid Vran heard how his messengers had been received he was determined somehow to make his peace with Matholwch, and he sent more messengers, this time led by his own brother Manawyddan, to beg the King to return in peace. "Tell him that he shall have a sound horse for every one that has been injured," he said, "and besides that, to make up for the insult, he shall have a silver staff as large and as tall as himself, and a plate of gold as broad as his face. And tell him that we have found out who it was that did the wicked deed unknown to me; but that as it was my half-brother, a son of Llyr, it would not be right for me to put him to death. Beg Matholwch once more to come and meet me, and we will make peace in any way he wishes."

So Manawyddan came to Matholwch, and when the Irish King heard what Bendigeid Vran had to say, he took counsel with his men, who advised him to accept the apology, and Matholwch returned to the Island of the Mighty.

Great were the rejoicings, and once again the tents were laid with a magnificent feast; but it seemed to Bendigeid Vran that his guest was not as happy as he had been before, and was perhaps worrying that the gifts were not big enough to atone for so great an insult.

"If that is so," he said, "I will add to them whatever you may wish. Tomorrow you shall have the horses, and I will also give you a magic cauldron. If one of your men should be slain, and the following day you throw his body into the cauldron, he will come out alive and well except that he will not be able to speak."

This delighted Matholwch. He thanked his host, and the feast continued with general rejoicing.

The next morning Bendigeid Vran ordered that all the horses that could be found should be handed over to Matholwch, and as there were not enough at Aberffraw to replace those which had been damaged, the whole Court travelled to another part of the country where there were sufficient colts to make up the right number, and another feast was held on the second night, at which the two kings talked together in great friendliness.

"My lord," said Matholwch, "where did you get the cauldron which you have given to me?"

"I had it from a man who came from your country," answered Bendigeid Vran, "and I would never have parted with it except to someone from Ireland. He and his wife escaped from the Iron House in Ireland when it was made red hot around them, and fled to this country. I am surprised that you do not know about it."

"I will tell you all I know," said Matholwch. "One day when I was out hunting I came to the mound at the head of a lake called the Lake of the Cauldron, and I saw a huge, yellow-haired man coming from the lake with a cauldron upon his back. He was dreadful to look at, and he was followed by a woman who was twice as large as he was. They came forward and greeted me, and I asked them where they were going. 'At the end of six weeks this woman will have a son,' said the man, 'and he will be no child, but a warrior fully armed.' So I took them home with me and saw that they were cared for, and they were with me for a year. I was glad to do what I could for them, but my people did not like it. For, after they had been with me three months, the two began to make themselves hated in the land, molesting and harassing my nobles and their ladies.

"My people rose up and begged that I would get rid of the strangers, telling me to choose between these interlopers and my country. But the man and his wife refused to go; so I called a council to seek advice as to what I should do. But my subjects took the law into their own hands and built a huge hall of iron. When it was finished every blacksmith in the country and every man who owned tongs and hammers came together and built a wall of coals round the hall, piled as high as the iron walls. In this hall of iron they spread a feast of meat and much drink for the man and woman and their family. As soon as they had drunk the wine and were overcome by it my countrymen lit the coals that were outside the walls and blew them up with bellows into a roaring fire till the iron walls were red-hot. Then, roused by the great heat, the man dashed against the door of the building and broke his way out, his wife following him; but they were the only ones who escaped. And then, I suppose," he said, "they came over here."

"Certainly they came here," said Bendigeid Vran, "and he gave the cauldron to me."

"How did you receive him?"

"I let them stay here, and as their family increased I spread them throughout my kingdom, and they have become numerous and have prospered, fortifying the country wherever they are with men and arms of the best that were ever seen."

And so the banquet went on long into the night, and the next day Matholwch left for Ireland with Branwen his bride.

Great was the rejoicing when he reached his own country, and royal was the welcome Branwen received. To every one of the nobles and ladies who visited her Branwen gave a ring or clasp or some royal jewel, and she was much honoured and loved by her husband's people. At the end of the year her son was born, and he was called Gwern son of Matholwch.

Branwen in Ireland

THE year after Branwen's son was born unrest grew up in the country of Ireland. There was much murmuring and discontent among the people because of the insult which their King had received in Britain when he went there to seek his bride. His foster-brother and the chief nobles blamed Matholwch because he had not taken vengeance for the disgrace which he had endured. Before long they became so angry that they rose up, drove Branwen from her position as Queen, and forced her to become a mere servant in the palace and do the cooking for the Court. And they made the butcher, when he delivered the meat each day, give her a blow on the ear as punishment for the wrongs their King had endured. And in case the news of Branwen's disgrace should reach her brother Bendigeid Vran they persuaded Matholwch to forbid any ships to go from Ireland to Britain, and if any travellers should come from Britain that they should be imprisoned and not allowed to go back: and this continued for three years.

So Branwen had no hope of news of her sad plight reaching her brother. But at last, imprisoned as she was in the kitchen of the palace, she managed to tame a young starling, which she reared in the kneading-trough. She taught the bird to speak, and told it about her brother and where he lived and what he was like. When the bird was full-grown she wrote a letter to Bendigeid Vran, telling him of the trouble she was in, bound the letter under the starling's wing and sent it off to fly to Britain.

The starling rose into the air and flew on until it came to the Island of the Mighty, and at last found Bendigeid Vran. It settled on his shoulder and ruffled its feathers so that the letter could be seen, and Bendigeid Vran understood that it was no common starling but a bird which had been carefully reared and trained. So he took the letter from its wing, and when he read it he was very grieved at the story of his sister's troubles. At once he sent out messengers throughout Britain to summon the islanders together that he might consult the mightiest in the land: and when they heard of the fate of Branwen they resolved to go in force to Ireland, leaving behind them seven princes to look after the kingdom while they were away. And the chief among these was Caradawc son of Bran.

So Bendigeid Vran sailed to Ireland with an army of many mighty warriors. As they neared the coast they came into shallow waters caused by the meeting of two rivers. Then Bendigeid Vran left his boat and proceeded through the water, with his provisions on his back, towards the land.

The approach of his ships was seen by some Irish swineherds on the shore, who hurried to tell Matholwch their King.

"Lord, we have wonderful news!" they cried. "We have seen a wood upon the sea in a place where never before was a single tree."

Matholwch was astonished, and asked them if they had noticed anything else that was strange.

"Indeed, Lord!" said the swineherds. "We saw a vast mountain beside the wood, and there was a high ridge on the top of the mountain and a lake on each side of the ridge, and all these things moved. They seemed to come from the direction of Britain."

"The only person who can know anything of this will be Branwen," said Matholwch, and he sent messengers to her in her kitchen.

"Lady," they said when they had told her what had been seen, "what do you think these things can be?"

"The men of the Island of the Mighty," said Branwen, "who have come here to bring vengeance for the way I have been treated."

"But what is the forest that is seen upon the sea?" they asked her.

"The masts of my brother's ships," she answered.

"And what is the mountain that is seen by the side of the ships?"

"Bendigeid Vran, my brother," she replied, "coming to shallow water. There is no ship that can hold him when the water is not deep."

"What is the high ridge with a lake on each side of it?"

"On looking towards this island he is angry, and his two eyes, one on each side of his nose, are the two lakes beside the ridge."

Then Matholwch quickly called together his warriors and took counsel as to what he should do.

"Lord," said his nobles, "there is only one thing to be done, and that is to retreat over the river Linon and keep this between thee and him, breaking down the bridge when we have all passed over it, for the loadstone at the bottom of the river will prevent any ship from crossing the water." And this they did in all haste.

Soon Bendigeid Vran came to land and led his troops towards the river Linon. His chieftains warned him of the loadstone, and that there was no bridge anywhere on the river.

"He who will be chief among us, let him be the bridge," said Bendigeid Vran. "I will be so." And he lay down across the river, and hurdles were placed on him, and so his warriors crossed over.

As soon as his army was safely on the far side Bendigeid Vran rose to his feet and was greeted by messengers from Matholwch. They welcomed him in a most friendly way in the name of their King, his own kinsman, and pointed out that Matholwch deserved nothing but good at his hands. "For Matholwch has given his kingdom to his son Gwern, your own nephew, the son of your own sister. And Matholwch himself is willing to live wherever you shall wish, either in Ireland or in your kingdom of Britain."

But Bendigeid Vran answered them: "Shall not I have the kingdom of Ireland for myself and my people? I will take counsel, and until I have done so I will give you no answer."

The messengers replied that they would tell Matholwch what he had said and would return quickly.

When they again reached their King they begged that he would send a better message to Bendigeid Vran: "For he will not listen to anything we could say." And when Matholwch asked them what they would advise, the messengers said: "Lord, there seems to us only one thing to be done. Bendigeid Vran is so great that there has never been a house that could hold him. Will you not build him one so vast that it would have room for him and the army he has brought on the one side, and yourself and your warriors on the other side? If you were to do this and also give your kingdom to him and do him homage, then he would make peace with you and we should be saved."

So great was the danger that Matholwch was willing to do this, and he sent the messengers back to Bendigeid Vran, who agreed to make peace on these terms.

So the Irish set to work to build the house, in which they planned to place a hundred pillars, each supported by two brackets. And they schemed among themselves, and on each bracket they hung a leather bag large enough to hold a man, and in each bag was an armed warrior.

The first to come into the house was Evnissyen, and looking round it, he saw the leather bags hanging up.

"What is in this bag?" he asked when he came to the first one.

"Meal, my lord," said one of the Irishmen.

Then Evnissyen touched the bag and felt round it till he came to the warrior's head; then with all his strength he squeezed till the head was crushed and the warrior was dead. He then went on from one bag to the next till he had been round them all, and each time he asked the same question and, receiving the same answer, he killed the warriors one by one and did not stop until all the two hundred men were dead.

After than Bendigeid Vran and his host entered the house on the one side, and Matholwch and his fighting-men on the other.

As soon as they sat down to the feast there was peace between them, and the kingdom of Ireland was handed over to Branwen's son, Gwern.

When the feast was over Bendigeid Vran called the boy to him, and from him Gwern went to his other uncle, Manawyddan and then on to Nissyen, and they all loved him, and so did everyone that saw him. Then Evnissyen called out: "Why does not my nephew come to me?"

"Certainly let him come to you," said Bendigeid Vran, and Gwern went to him without fear. Then Evnissyen got up, seized Gwern by his feet, and before anyone could stop him he thrust the boy head first into the blazing fire.

When Branwen saw what was happening, she would have leapt into the flames to try to save her son, but Bendigeid Vran held her firmly and would not let her go. Then was there a great commotion in the house. Bendigeid Vran supported Branwen with his shield, while all the warriors on each side of the house hastened to arm themselves, and loud was the tumult and clash of arms. The Irish quickly kindled a fire under the cauldron and threw in the bodies of their warriors who had been killed fighting and also the men in the sacks until it was full, and the next day they came out, alive and well except that they could not speak. But the fighting men of Britain who had been slain remained dead, and there was no way of reviving them.

When Evnissyen saw this he called out: "Woe is me that I should have been the cause of betraying our own army. I must find a way of saving all that are left," and he flung himself down among the dead of the enemy. As he lay there the Irish, thinking him to be one of their own dead, picked him up and tossed him into the cauldron, and Evnissyen stretched himself out till the cauldron burst into four pieces; but he himself was dead.

This gave time for Bendigeid Vran's army to rally a little; but they were unable to beat the Irish for only seven men were left out of their whole army. And among the seven who escaped, besides Bendigeid Vran himself, were his brother Manawyddan and Pryderi son of Pwyll.

Then Bendigeid Vran commanded that they should cut off his head and take it back to the White Mount in London, where they were to bury it with the face towards France.

"You will be a long time on the way," he said. "For seven years you will feast at Harlech, and the birds of Rhiannon, mother of Pryderi, will sing to you: and all the time my head will be as pleasant company to you as ever it was on my body. And you will stay for eighty years at Gwales, until you open the door that faces towards Cornwall. But once that door is open you may rest no longer but must hurry on towards London."

His followers did as he commanded and set sail for Britain, taking Branwen with them. In despair she looked first at the land of her birth and then at Ireland, crying out: "Alas that I was ever born! Two islands have been destroyed because of me," and in great sorrow she died, and they buried her beside the river Alaw.

Then the seven men, bearing with them the head of Bendigeid Vran, travelled on to Harlech, and as they went they met a crowd of people and stopped to ask them if there was any news.

"We know none," a man told them, "except that Caswallawn the son of Beli has conquered the Island of the Mighty and is crowned King in London."

"What has become of Caradawc and the princes who were left in charge of the land?"

"Six of them were slain by Caswallawn, and Caradawc their chief died of grief because, though he could see the sword that killed his comrades, he could not make out who it was that wielded it; for Caswallawn had hidden himself in the Veil of Illusion and was invisible."

So the seven men continued their journey to Harlech, where they stopped to rest themselves and take food. And there came three birds who sang to them songs that were more beautiful than any they had ever heard; and they remained at Harlech for seven years before they travelled on to Gwales.

At Gwales they found a spacious hall built in a beautiful spot overlooking the sea. There were three doors in the hall, two of which were open; but the third, which looked towards Cornwall, was closed.

"This is surely the door we must not open," said Manawyddan, and that night they held a feast and were joyful. And when they had eaten they remembered nothing of the feast, nor of anything that had happened to them in the past, and for eighty years they remained in Gwales. The time passed in great happiness, and no man knew how long he had remained there, and the head of Bendigeid Vran seemed to them as if it were their King himself, alive and well, and great was their rejoicing.

At the end of this time Heilyn, who was one of their number, grew curious about the shut door and opened it and looked towards Cornwall. As soon as they had all looked through the door the seven men remembered everything, especially the fate of Bendigeid Vran and the loss of all their friends in Ireland. So sorrowful were they that they could no longer rest, but hurried forward with the head towards London. And they buried the head of Bendigeid Vran in the White Mount, which some think was the Tower of London, with the face turned towards France: and while the head remained there no invasion could come to the Island of the Mighty from over the sea.

Meanwhile in Ireland no man was left alive, only five women who were each about to have a child, and these lived together in a cave. And in the same night a son was born to each one of the women, and the boys grew up and thrived. When they were men they divided the land between them, and they found riches where the battle-field had been, and grew wealthy and prospered. And they named the five divisions of Ireland Munster, Leinster, Connaught, Ulster and Meath.

Manawyddan the Son of Llyr

WHEN Manawyddan, with his six companions who had escaped from the war in Ireland, had buried the head of his brother, Bendigeid Vran, in the White Mount of London, a great sadness came upon him, for he felt that he had no longer any place in the kingdom.

"Do not despair, my lord," said Pryderi son of Pwyll, who had travelled with him from Ireland. "Though by rights you should be our King you have never been ambitious, and he who rules here now is no stranger but your own cousin Caswallawn the son of Beli."

"That I know," answered Manawyddan, "but though he is my cousin it grieves me to know that he has taken the place of my brother Bendigeid Vran."

"I think I could help you," said Pryderi. "I still own the country of Dyved, where my mother Rhiannon lives with Kicva my wife. When Rhiannon was young she was the fairest in the land, and even now she is considered very beautiful and wise. I will give her to you in marriage and the kingdom of Dyved with her, and there is no fairer country in all the land."

"May Heaven reward thee for thy friendship," said Manawyddan. "I will come with you at once and meet Rhiannon and look at your possessions."

They set out without delay, and when at last they came to Narberth, which was the chief palace in Pryderi's country of Dyved, they found a feast prepared for them by Rhiannon and Kicva. Manawyddan sat beside Rhiannon and talked with her, and greatly did he admire her both for her conversation and her beauty. At length, turning to his friend, he spoke.

"Pryderi, let it be as you said!"

"What was it that he said?" asked Rhiannon.

"Lady," said Pryderi, "I offered to give your hand in marriage to Manawyddan, son of Llyr."

This pleased Rhiannon, who had taken a great liking to Manawyddan, and she agreed gladly to the proposal.

"I, too, am greatly pleased," said he. "May Heaven prosper him who hath shown me such perfect friendship."

So Rhiannon became his bride amidst great rejoicing and feasting. And they journeyed through the land that Manawyddan might see the country that was now his, and he thought that he had never seen lands more pleasant to live in, with excellent hunting grounds and plenty of honey and fish. Great was the friendship between himself and his bride and Pryderi and Kicva, and they travelled together wherever they went and never wished to be separated.

After a little time Pryderi left them and went to do homage to the new king, Caswallawn, at Oxford, where he was well received and praised for coming. When he returned great was his welcome, and again there was feasting at Narberth.

When the feast was over and the servants who had waited upon them were taking their food, Pryderi led his mother and his wife with Manawyddan to the royal mound of Narberth, and with them went their courtiers. As they sat there a great storm came up. Thunder pealed above them, and lightning flashed, and with the storm came a mist so thick that nothing could be seen and no man could make out where his companions sat. When the mist lifted and it grew light the four could see each other again; but there was no sign of any other man. They looked over the countryside where there had been cattle and herds, but these too had vanished, and now there was nothing there. Gone was the farmhouse, and there was no sign of man nor beast, smoke nor fire. Nothing remained but the houses of the Court, and these were empty and deserted. No living thing could they see, but only their four selves.

"Where are the men of the Court, and also my own following?" cried Manawyddan. "Let us go and seek for them!"

So they hunted over the castle and the hall, the mead-cellar and the kitchens, but nowhere could they find anything but desolation. Though they searched through the whole country, they could see nothing but deserted dwellings and wild beasts. But the four were still together, and they did not despair. When their food was finished they lived on the prey which they killed in hunting and the honey of the wild bees, and in this way two years passed pleasantly enough; but after that they began to grow tired of the life.

"We cannot go on living like this," said Manawyddan. "Let us go to a town and learn some trade by which we can keep ourselves."

So they travelled to Hereford and settled down to make saddles. And Manawyddan began to make housings also, which were the cloth coverings for horses, and he gilded and coloured both these and the saddles with blue enamel. So great was their success that everyone came to buy their saddles and housings, and none other was sold in Hereford.

Then the saddlers in the town met together to see what could be done, as they were no longer able to sell their own goods, and they decided to kill the four who were taking all their trade from them. But warning was brought to Manawyddan that he should leave the town at once.

"Let us not run away," said Pryderi. "It would be better that we should stay and fight these ruffians."

But Manawyddan did not agree. "If we fight with them and kill them, we shall be looked upon as wicked men and thrown into prison. It will be better for us to go to another town and there settle down to earn our livings." So they left Hereford and went on to another city.

"This time we will make shields," said Manawyddan.

"Do we know anything of this craft?" asked Pryderi.

"We will try," answered Manawyddan. So they began to make shields, shaping them like the good shields they had seen and enamelling them as they had the saddles. And so great was their success that their shields were the best in the town, and no one would buy any but the shields they made.

Once again the craftsmen of the town came together and agreed that the newcomers must be slain, for otherwise there was no trade left for anyone else. Again the four received a warning, and again Pryderi wished to stay and fight for their rights.

"This we cannot do," said Manawyddan, "or Caswallawn and his men will hear of it and we shall be undone. Let us go to another town."

This time they decided to make shoes. "For maybe there is not courage enough among cobblers to fight us or to molest us."

"But I know nothing of the making of shoes," said Pryderi.

"I know, and I will teach you to stitch," answered Manawyddan. "We will not attempt to dress the leather, but we will buy it ready dressed and make the shoes from it."

So they bought the best leather that could be found in the town and learned from the best goldsmiths how to make gold buckles and clasps for their own shoes, and they came to be called the Makers of Gold Shoes. Once again their success was so great that their goods were sought before all others, and when the cobblers of the town found that they could sell none of their own shoes, they called a meeting and decided that they must kill the interlopers; but again a warning was given to the four. Again Pryderi wished to stay and fight it out; but again Manawyddan persuaded him to leave.

"Let us go back to Dyved," he said, so they travelled on till they came to the deserted castle of Narberth. There they kindled a fire and supported themselves by hunting, and stayed there in contentment for a year.

One morning when Manawyddan and Pryderi were out hunting with their dogs they came to a bush, and the dogs quickly drew away from it, their hair bristling, and returned to their masters. The men rode forward, and in the bush they found a wild boar of pure white, and set their dogs on it. The boar fell back, then turned and held the dogs at bay till the men came up. Then it fell back a second time, and this time fled from the hunting party. The men took up the chase; but the boar ran quickly and, coming suddenly to a castle where before no castle had been, ran swiftly into it, the dogs following. The men drew rein and listened; but no sound of the dogs could be heard.

"Lord," said Pryderi, "I will follow the dogs into the castle."

"Do not be so unwise," said Manawyddan. "Someone has cast a spell over this land and caused the castle to be here."

But Pryderi did not want to lose his dogs, and in spite of this advice he hurried into the castle. But when he got inside he could see no sign of either dogs or boar. Everything was deserted; but in the centre of the castle floor was a fountain surrounded by marble work on which stood a golden bowl of great beauty upon a marble slab, and chains hung from the air, the ends of which could not be seen. The gold was so wonderfully wrought that Pryderi went up and touched it. At once his hand stuck to the bowl and his feet to the slab on which he stood, and he found that he could not speak nor make any sound.

Meanwhile Manawyddan waited outside the castle till evening fell; then he returned to the palace and told Rhiannon what had happened.

"A poor friend you have been to my son," said Rhiannon, "to leave him alone without help," and she went out at once and hurried towards the castle. As before, the gate stood open, and going in she found Pryderi still standing beside the bowl.

"Oh my Lord," she cried, "what are you doing here?" and going up to him she took hold of the bowl. At once her hand became fixed to it and her feet to the slab, and she too was unable to speak or make any sound, and there they remained. As night fell there came a thunder-storm and with it a mist, and the castle, with Rhiannon and Pryderi inside it, disappeared from the countryside.

When the news was brought to Kicva she was so grieved that she did not care whether she lived or died, and she feared to be left alone with Manawyddan.

"Do not be afraid," he said. "I will ever keep my faith with Pryderi and with you. But we have lost our dogs so I cannot hunt, and we shall not be able to get food. Let us go again to Lloegyr where it will be easier to make a livelihood."

So to Lloegyr they went, and once more Manawyddan settled down to the trade of making shoes, which he did for a year with the same success as before. Once again the cobblers conspired to kill him because he had taken all their trade, and once more he and Kicva escaped and went back to Narberth, this time taking with them as much wheat as they could carry.

At Narberth Manawyddan fished and hunted, and they lived on what he was able to catch: and he prepared the ground of three fields and sowed the wheat they had brought. The wheat grew well, and never had there been seen better, and when the harvest time came Manawyddan saw that the first crop was bountiful.

"I will reap this tomorrow," he said, and went back to Narberth. But when the morning came he found that nothing was left of his wheat but the bare straw, all the ears having vanished from their stalks. So he went to look at the second field, which also he found to be ripe and ready for harvesting. "I will reap this tomorrow," he said; but again when the next day came nothing was left of the crop, only the bare straw.

"Alas!" he cried, "Whoever it is that has begun my ruin is completing it, and has also destroyed the country with me," and he went to look at the third crop, which he found to be ripe and even finer than the other two had been. So he hurried back to the castle and told Kicva all that had happened.

"Whoever carried off the grain from the first two fields will come tonight to take this," he said. "Tonight I will watch the crop and lie in wait that I may find out who it is," and arming himself he went to watch the field.

At midnight there was the loudest tumult that he had ever heard, and looking up he saw a great host of mice, so many that he could not count or even guess at their number. They rushed upon the wheat and, each of them climbing up a straw which bent down under its weight, cut off one of the ears and carried it away, and in all the field there was not a single stalk that had not a mouse on it. Before he could move they had all turned and rushed away at such a speed that he could not come up with them; but one mouse was slower than the rest and, running fast, Manawyddan managed to catch it. He put it in his glove, tied the opening with string and took it back with him to the palace.

"What have you there, my lord?" asked Kicva when she saw the glove.

"A thief," said Manawyddan, and told her the story of the mice and how his last crop of wheat had been destroyed. "But one mouse was less nimble than the rest," he said, "and tomorrow I will hang it."

"My lord," said Kicva, "this is indeed wonderful. But surely it is beneath your dignity that you should be hanging a low creature like a mouse. Would it not be better to let it go?"

"I would hang the lot if I could catch them," he answered her, "and this one I have caught, and it shall hang."

"I have no reason to help it except to save your dignity," she said, "so I willingly agree that you must do as you wish with it."

Then Manawyddan went to the royal mound of Narberth, taking the mouse with him in the glove, and he set up two forks on the highest part of the hill. While he was doing this he saw a scholar coming towards him, dressed in rags, which surprised him greatly since he had seen no living person in Dyved except their four selves for the last seven years.

They exchanged greetings, and he asked the scholar where he had come from.

"I have been singing in Lloegyr," said the scholar. "But why do you ask?"

So Manawyddan told him of the curse on the land, and that he had seen no human since the night of the storm and mist.

"I am but travelling through the land on the way to my own country," said the scholar. "May I ask what you are doing?"

"I am hanging a thief which I caught robbing me."

"What kind of a thief is that?" asked the scholar. "I see a mouse in your hand. Surely a man of your rank and dignity should not touch such vermin. Let it go free!"

This Manawyddan refused to do.

"Lord," urged the scholar, "rather than see you so demean yourself I will give you this pound, which I received as alms, if you will let the creature go."

"I will neither let it go nor sell it," answered Manawyddan.

"As you will. I care not, except that I do not like to see a man of your rank touching anything so low," and the scholar went his way.

As Manawyddan was placing the cross-bar on the two forks a priest, riding on a horse covered with trappings, came towards him.

"Good-day to thee," called out the priest.

Manawyddan returned the greeting and asked the priest for his blessing, which he gave.

"And what are you doing?" asked the priest.

"I am hanging a thief which I caught robbing me," said Manawyddan. "It is a mouse, and deserves its doom."

"Lord," answered the priest, "rather than see you defile yourself by touching such a creature I will give you three pounds to let it go."

"I will not take any price for it. It ought to be hanged, and so it shall be."

"Do as you will, my lord," replied the priest and went his way.

Manawyddan made a noose of the string and slipped it round the mouse's neck; but before he could draw it up he saw a bishop, followed by his retinue, all mounted on fine horses, coming towards him.

"Lord bishop, give me thy blessing," he said.

This the bishop gave, then he asked Manawyddan what he was doing, and Manawyddan answered as he had before.

"Since I have come up at the doom of this creature I will ransome it of thee. I will give you seven pounds rather than see a man of thy rank destroying so vile an animal."

"I declare to Heaven that I will not set it loose," said Manawyddan.

The bishop then offered him twenty-four pounds, and when Manawyddan again refused, he again made an offer. "I will give you all the horses that you can see on this plain, and seven loads of baggage and the seven horses that carry the baggage if you will let the creature go," and when Manawyddan again refused, the bishop asked him to name whatever he wished as a price for the freedom of the mouse.

"I wish that Rhiannon and Pryderi shall be freed," said Manawyddan.

"That wish you shall have," answered the bishop. "Now set the mouse free."

"Not yet, by Heaven," said Manawyddan. "Not until the curse be removed from the country of Dyved."

"This also you shall have," the bishop agreed. "Now let the mouse go."

"Not yet," said Manawyddan again. "I must know who the mouse is."

"She is my wife," answered the bishop.

"And I must know why she came to me."

"She came to despoil thee. For I am Llwyd the son of Kilcoed, and I put the curse on the country of Dyved to avenge my friend Gwawl the son of Clud. I put a charm on Pryderi as a vengeance for the indignity of the game of Badger in the Bag, which his father Pwyll played upon Gwawl at the court of Heveydd Hên. When it was known that you were come to live in the land my household asked that I would turn them into mice that they might destroy thy corn. It was my household that went the first night and stole your crop, and also the second night. And the third night my wife came and the ladies of the Court and begged that I would turn them also into mice, which I did. My wife is about to have a child, which is why she was less nimble than the rest and you were able to catch her. But as you have her in your power I will restore Pryderi and Rhiannon to you and will take the curse off the country of Dyved. Now you know who she is, therefore set her free."

"I will not set her free, by Heaven," declared Manawyddan.

"What more do you want?" asked the bishop.

"I wish for a pledge that never again shall there be a curse put on the country of Dyved."

"This I will promise," said the bishop. "Now set her free."

"By my faith I will not till I have your promise that vengeance shall never be taken for this, either upon Pryderi or Rhiannon or upon me."

"This you shall have, too," promised the bishop, "and wise you were to ask it, for on your head would have come much trouble. Now, having all your wishes granted, set my wife free."

"I will not," said Manawyddan, "until I see Rhiannon and Pryderi with my own eyes."

"Behold, here they come," answered the bishop.

Then Pryderi and Rhiannon came walking over the plain, free and well, and greeted Manawyddan: and when the bishop again asked for the release of his wife Manawyddan gladly agreed, and the mouse was let loose.

Then Llwyd struck her with a magic wand, and she changed back into a young woman of great beauty.

"What bondage has been laid upon Pryderi and Rhiannon?" asked Manawyddan.

"Pryderi has had the knockers of the gates of my palace about his neck, and Rhiannon has had the collars of the asses after they have been carrying hay about hers," said Llwyd. "But now look around at your land, and you will see it tilled and peopled."

And Manawyddan looked and saw that all was well and the country fair and prosperous as it had been before the curse had been laid upon it.

A TALE OF LLUDD SON OF BELI

Lludd and Llevelys

I N the long ago days the Bards sang of a King of Britain called Beli the Great and of his son Lludd, who ruled after him. Lludd was a famous soldier and a good king. He ruled well and wisely, built many fine houses and also rebuilt the walls of London, where he liked best to live. He had three brothers, Caswallawn, Nynaw, and the youngest, Llevelys, who had a gift of great wisdom so that he could see and understand things that were hidden from other men.

One day Llevelys came to Lludd with news that the King of France had died and had left his kingdom and all his possessions to his daughter. This princess Llevelys wanted to marry, so that the two countries might be united in friendship, and he came to his brother to ask for ships and men that he might go to France in a style worthy of so great a mission. Lludd was glad to give him all the help he could, and Llevelys went to France, married the princess, and they lived happily together and governed France with great wisdom and justice.

It was some time after this that three plagues fell on the country of Britain of a kind that had never been heard of before, and nothing King Lludd could do would rid his kingdom of them.

The first plague was an invasion by the Coranians, a race of people who had the magic power of hearing whatever was said on the island, however privately. Men might speak in whispers or behind closed doors, but their words were always caught up by the wind and carried away to the Coranians. When Lludd conferred with the leaders of his army the wind bore his words to the ears of the enemy, and when the leaders of the army in turn gave orders to their men,the Coranians in a moment knew all that had been said. In this way the invaders were never in danger of a surprise attack. They knew just what the Britons were about to do, and they could never be defeated.

The second plague, though it came only once a year, was even worse. On the eve of every May Day the peace of the land was shattered by a piercing shriek, which rang through the island from sea to sea. The sound of it was so terrifying that strong men paled and lost their strength, while old and young alike lost their senses with fear, and even the animals and the trees, the earth and the waters were stricken: and no one could discover the cause of the dreadful sound.

The third plague fell on the Court of the King. When food was cooked for the Court, however large the banquet, however much was prepared and laid before the King and his courtiers, once they had finished their meal nothing was ever seen again of what was left in the castle. However large the bakings, however big the catering orders, even when enough was laid in to last for a year ahead, still nothing was left of it the following morning.

These three plagues brought great sorrow to King Lludd, and he called together the nobles of the land to ask their advice. A great council was held, and after much discussion the nobles advised the King to call on the help of his brother, the King of France. So Lludd summoned a large fleet of ships, and taking with him the chief warriors of the country he sailed over the Channel to France.

On hearing of the great fleet nearing his shores, King Llevelys in his turn gathered a mighty navy together for fear lest the approaching ships might be coming to attack his country, and he himself came to the coast to meet them.

When Lludd was told of this he left his fleet far out at sea and sailed towards the land in a single ship. Then Llevelys came to meet him and give him welcome, and there was much rejoicing between the two brothers who had not met for many years. And Lludd told Llevelys of the dreadful troubles that had fallen on the land of Britain, and asked him for the help of his great wisdom. But as soon as he started talking of the Coranians and their magic powers Llevelys stopped him and would not let him speak for fear the wind should pick up their words and carry them away to the enemy. And Llevelys ordered a long horn of brass to be made through which they could talk to each other in safety. But at first there was trouble, for a demon got into the horn and changed the words as they came, so that each king heard nothing but harsh and hostile talk. So Llevelys called for wine to wash out the horn and so drove the demon away, and the two kings could speak to each other through the horn undisturbed.

Then Llevelys told his brother that he would give him some insects which Lludd must put into water, and that the water would then have the power to destroy the Coranians and would at the same time be powerless to harm the men of the island of Britain. And he advised Lludd to keep back some of the insects lest later on there should be another invasion.

"When you come again to your kingdom," said Llevelys, "call together a great meeting of the people, both of your own subjects and of the Coranians, as though you wished to make peace between the two peoples. And when they are collected together, then take the charmed water and throw it over the whole crowd gathered before you, and such is the magic in the water that the Coranians will die of the poisoning, but your own people shall be unharmed."

Greatly cheered by his brother's words, Lludd then told him of the terrible shrieking that had filled Britain and done so much harm to the people. What could be the cause of so dreadful a sound?

"There is a dragon in your country," answered Llevelys, "and it is being attacked by another, a foreign dragon that is trying to kill it and causing it to shriek so that all the country hears and is devastated."

At this Lludd was much concerned. "But how am I to find

the dragons," he cried, "and put an end to the fighting?"

"You must measure your kingdom from the north to the south, and again from the east to the west, and thus find out the exact centre of the land. There you must order a vast pit to be dug, and in the pit place a cauldron filled with the best mead in the land, and hide the cauldron beneath a covering of satin. This done, you must dismiss your men and alone you must keep watch. And you shall see two monstrous animals fighting: and as you watch they will rise into the air, and you will find that they are two dragons engaged in desperate battle. And at last, worn out by their furious fighting, they will fall through the air, changing as they come into two pigs: and you will see them fall on to the satin covering and sink down with it to the bottom of the cauldron, and they will drink the mead to the last drop, and when there is no more mead they will fall asleep. As soon as they sleep you must step forward, fold the satin covering round them and carry them away to the strongest part of the land and there bury them in a strong grave, and as long as they lie there no harm shall come to the island."

This also pleased Lludd greatly, and he made haste to tell his brother of the third plague, and of the mysterious disappearance of the provisions from the Court.

"This again you can cure," said Llevelys. "The thief is a powerful magician who causes a deep sleep to fall on all at your Court while he carries away your meat and your wine. And here again only you have the power to dispel his magic."

"And how is this to be done? I have set watches to protect my goods, but always they have been overcome by sleep."

"You must yourself keep watch as soon as the Court dinner is over. Have by your side a cauldron of cold water, so that when you feel a heavy drowsiness coming over you, you can plunge into the water. This will destroy the magic power, you will be able to keep awake and you will meet the magician face to face."

At this Lludd thanked his brother with much rejoicing, and

bidding him farewell called his men together and returned to Britain.

Once home he wasted no time in following the advice his brother had given him, and all happened just as Llevelys had foretold. First Lludd freed the country of the Coranian invaders, then he turned his attention to the shrieking dragon. The pit was dug at Oxford, which he found to be the exact centre of his kingdom, and Lludd watched the fight of the dragons and their fall in the form of pigs. As soon as they slept he wrapped the satin round them and carried them away to the wild crags of Snowdon, where he buried them in a stone grave, and all was quiet, and the terrible shrieks came no more to disturb the country.

Lludd then ordered a magnificent banquet to be prepared at the Court, and, arraying himself as for battle, he presided at the feast and commanded that a cauldron of cold water should be placed at his side. At the end of the banquet he watched his courtiers one by one fall asleep, and Lludd himself felt a great drowsiness come over him. But he remembered his brother's words and, plunging many times into the cold water, he managed to keep himself awake. And at last, while all the courtiers slept, through the door came a giant, fully armed and carrying a hamper. Round the table he went, putting all that was left of the food and wine into his hamper: and however much he put in,the hamper was never full, but always would hold more, till nothing was left of the feast.

As he turned to go Lludd stood up and called to the giant to stop. "Much harm have you done," he cried. "But now your thieving is at an end. Stand and defend yourself!"

Then the giant put down the hamper and awaited Lludd's attack, and great was the battle that followed. So fierce was their fighting that glittering fire flew out from their swords, till at last Lludd threw the thief to the ground, and the defeated giant begged for mercy.

"Why should I grant you mercy," asked Ludd, "when you have for so long wronged me and my country?"

Then the giant swore that he would pay back all that he had ever taken, and would give up his wicked ways. "And I will be your faithful servant from this time on."

And Ludd believed what the giant said, forgave and trusted him.

And so King Lludd, having freed the country from the dreadful plagues, ruled in peace and prosperity to the end of his days.

So sang the Bards of old, and today we still remember King Lludd. London itself bears his name, first called Caerlud, then Caer London, then London: and his burial place is still called Ludgate.

And five centuries later the dragons came back into our history when the enchanter Merlin caused the ground where they lay on Snowdon to be dug and the two sleeping dragons to be exposed. They woke, and at once went on with their fierce battle. At first the white dragon seemed to be getting the better of his foe; but at last the red dragon defeated him and drove him out of the country. And Merlin told the people that the red was the British dragon and the white the dragon of the invading Saxons, and to this day the Red Dragon is the national standard of the Welsh.

TALES OF THE KNIGHTS OF KING ARTHUR

Kilhwch and Olwen—The Search for Olwen

WHEN Kilhwch the son of Kilydd and cousin of King Arthur was but a baby, the Queen, his mother, became very ill. She called her husband to her and said to him: "Of this sickness I shall die, and you will take another wife." She then begged him, for their son's sake, not to marry again until he should see a briar growing on her grave with two blossoms on it. She also asked him to have her grave weeded every year, knowing that if this were done no plant could live.

For seven years Kilydd did as she wished; but after that he no longer had the grave tended as he had promised, and one day when he was out hunting he saw a briar growing on the grave. Then he felt that the time had come for him to seek another wife.

"I know a lady that will suit you well," said one of his counsellors. "She is the wife of King Doged."

The idea pleased the King, and thereupon he and his men set out for the land of King Doged, killed the King and brought away his wife and her daughter, conquering the lands as they went.

She and Kilydd were soon married. At first she hoped that her stepson Kilhwch would wed her own daughter; but the boy protested, saying that he was not yet old enough to marry. When she realized that he could not be persuaded she told him that it was his destiny that Olwen, the daughter of Yspaddaden Penkawr, should be his bride, and in such glowing terms did she speak of the lady that Kilhwch at once fell in love with Olwen, although he had never seen her.

Noticing his son's thoughtful air, his father asked him the cause of it, and when Kilhwch told him he said: "It will be easy for you to win her. King Arthur is your cousin and is all powerful. Go therefore and ask that he cut your hair, as is the custom when wishing to show a man great honour, and claim kinship. Then beg of him this boon."

So the youth rode away on his beautiful horse with a saddle of gold. In his hand he carried two spears of silver with steel heads so sharp that they could wound the wind. At his side was a golden sword, and before him went two brindle greyhounds with collars of rubies, and they ran from side to side and sported about his horse like two sea-swallows. He wore a four-cornered cloth of purple with an apple of gold at each corner, and his shoes and his stirrups were of gold. So light was his passage that the blades of grass did not bend under him as he rode towards the gate of Arthur's palace.

"Is there no porter here?" he asked of a man by the gate.

"There is," was the answer. "On the first day of January each year I am Arthur's porter, but on no other day. But you will not be welcome here unless you keep quiet; for there is revelry in Arthur's hall, and the King is at dinner."

"Open the gate!" cried Kilhwch.

The porter refused, saying that none might enter except the son of a king of a privileged country or a craftsman bringing his craft. "But there will be refreshment for your dogs and your horses, and a fine dinner for you and your men in the guest chamber where strangers and the sons of other countries eat. You will feast as well there as you would with King Arthur himself, and tomorrow morning the gate will be open to all who come, and you shall sit in Arthur's hall."

"That I will not do," said Kilhwch. "If you do not open this gate I will give three great shouts that will be heard from Land's End to the extreme north of Britain, and I will bring disgrace upon your lord and evil report upon you," and he threatened to call down a curse upon the palace if he were not allowed to enter.

At this the porter said he would tell the King himself, and went into the dining-hall.

"Have you news from the gate?" asked Arthur.

"I have indeed. In all my life and in all my travels I have never met a man with such great dignity as he who now waits at your gate."

Then Arthur said: "If you came here walking, then you go back to the gate running! Such a man must not be kept waiting in the wind and rain, and I command every man of you to show him respect and see that he is well served with meat and wine."

When Kilhwch heard Arthur's message all his men dismounted; but he himself rode forward on his charger into the hall.

"Greetings unto thee, sovereign ruler of this Island," he cried when he saw Arthur, and Arthur welcomed him and bade him sit down and join the revels.

"I did not come here to feast with you," replied Kilhwch, "but to crave a boon."

"Anything you ask shall be given to you," said the King, "except for my ship, my mantle, my arms, and my wife."

"I pray that you will bless my hair," answered Kilhwch.

Then Arthur took a golden comb and scissors of silver and combed Kilhwch's hair, and asked who he might be. "For my heart warms towards you," said the King, "and I feel that you are one of my own family." When Arthur heard that his guest was indeed his own cousin he again begged him to ask whatever boon he liked and it should be given to him.

"I beg of you that you will obtain for me the hand of Olwen, daughter of Yspaddaden Penkawr, in marriage. I ask this boon of you and of all the warriors who serve you."

"I have never heard of the maiden," replied Arthur, "but I will send messengers to look for her. Give me time, and I will find her for you."

"I will willingly give you time," said Kilhwch, "until one year from tonight."

So Kilhwch stayed on at the Court, while Arthur sent out messengers who travelled throughout his country; but at the end of twelve months they returned without any news of the lady they sought.

"Everyone who has come to you has received his boon except me," complained Kilhwch. "I shall leave your Court and consider you to be dishonoured for not keeping your word."

At this Kai, one of Arthur's warriors, cried out in shame that Kilhwch should have dared to reproach King Arthur. "Go with us," he said, "and we will not part till we have found the maiden or until you admit that she does not exist in this world."

This pleased the King, and he called five more of his knights, each of whom had a special gift, and told them to join Kai and Kilhwch in their search. First he called Bedwyr who, except for Arthur himself, was the swiftest in the land and, although one-handed, could beat three men in battle, while his lance would cause a wound equal to that of nine opposing lances. Next he called Kynddelig the Guide, who could find his way as well in a strange country as he could in his own. Third he called Gwrhyr, because he could speak all languages, and then his own nephew Gwalchmai, of whom it was said that he never failed in a quest nor returned home without that which he had gone out to seek. Lastly Arthur called out Menw, lest they should come into danger; for Menw could cast a charm over the whole party and make them invisible whenever he chose.

These knights set out with Kilhwch, and after much travelling they came to a vast plain in which stood a castle finer than any they had ever seen. The party rode forward quickly; but though for three days they journeyed towards it the castle remained as far away as ever. As they rode they came to a huge flock of sheep and their herdsman, who was sitting on a mound. By his side sat a shaggy mastiff, larger than a horse, a savage dog who, though he protected the sheep so well that none had ever been lost, delighted to do harm to others. So fiery was his breath that it had burned down all the trees and bushes of the plain.

Then Kai rode forward with Gwrhyr to speak to the herdsman, while Menw cast a spell upon the dog so that it should become harmless.

When greetings had been exchanged they asked the herdsman whose were the sheep that he tended, and to whom the beautiful castle belonged.

"You must be very ignorant," answered the herdsman, "for all the world know that this is the castle of Yspaddaden Penkawr. He is my brother, but he has brought me low because of my great possessions. And who may you be?"

"We are an embassy from King Arthur, and we come to seek Olwen, your brother's daughter."

"May Heaven have mercy on you," said the herdsman. "You must give up this quest, for no one who ever came to court the daughter of Yspaddaden Penkawr has returned alive."

Then Kilhwch made friends with the herdsman, whose name was Custennin, and gave him a golden ring, and before they parted, Custennin asked them all to come to his home that evening.

"Who is the man who gave you the ring?" asked his wife.

"He is Kilhwch the son of Kilydd, and he has come to seek the hand of our niece Olwen in marriage."

At this his wife was both filled with joy at the thought that she would be seeing Kilhwch, for he was the son of her own sister, and at the same time very sorrowful that he had come on such a dangerous quest, for she knew that many had sought the hand of Olwen but none had returned alive.

As the party approached Custennin's home his wife ran out eagerly to welcome them, and was about to fling her arms round Kai's neck when he seized a log and thrust it between her hands. In her joy at seeing them she squeezed it so fiercely that it became a twisted coil, and Kai cried out: "If you had squeezed me thus it would have been the last embrace I should ever have had."

They went into the house and were made welcome, and as they were getting ready for dinner the herdsman's wife went to the chimney corner and opened a stone chest, and out of it stepped a young boy with fair, curling hair.

"Why does he have to stay hidden in that chest?" asked Gwrhyr.

"This is the last of my children," said the woman sadly. "Twenty-three of my sons have been slain by Yspaddaden Penkawr, and I fear that he will kill this one also."

"Let him come with me," said Kai, "and I promise you that as long as I live he shall not be slain."

Then the woman tried to persuade the party to give up their quest and return to their homes while still there was time. But this, Kai told her, they would never do, and he asked if the fair Olwen ever came to the house they were in.

"She comes here every Saturday to wash her hair, and always she leaves her rings in the basin and never comes back to fetch them."

"Would she come here if you sent for her?"

"That I will never do unless you give me your word that no harm shall come to her."

"We promise you that none shall harm her," said Kai, and Custennin's wife sent off a message to the castle.

Then Olwen came. She was dressed in flame-coloured silk with a collar of gold studded with emeralds and rubies, and her hair was more yellow than the flower of the broom, her skin whiter than the foam of the wave, and fairer were her hands and fingers than the blossoms of the wood-anemone. No hawk or falcon had brighter eyes than she, and her cheeks were redder than the reddest rose. Four white trefoils sprung up wherever she trod, and none could see the maiden without loving her.

She came in and sat on a bench beside Kilhwch.

The Winning of Olwen

As Kilhwch gazed at Olwen he knew at once that she was the maiden he had loved for so long, and he begged her to come away with him without delay.

"I cannot," she answered, "for I have promised my father not to wed without his consent; for when I marry he will die. You must first obtain his permission, and whatever he asks of you you must do. If you deny him anything you will fail to win me, and you will be lucky if you escape with your life."

Kilhwch promised that he would do all she said, and Olwen returned alone to her home. The knights followed and when they came to the castle they found that it was guarded by a porter and a watch-dog at each of its nine gates. These they slew in silence, without a single watch-dog having time to bark, and they went forward into the hall.

There sat Yspaddaden Penkawr, and the knights gave him greetings suitable to a great nobleman.

"Why have you come?" asked Yspaddaden Penkawr.

"We come to ask the hand of your daughter Olwen for Kilhwch the son of Kilydd."

Then Yspaddaden Penkawr called to his servants and commanded them to raise up the forks between his eyebrows that he might see the man who would be his son-in-law.

"Come back tomorrow," he said, "and you shall have your answer," but as they went he picked up one of the three poisoned darts that lay beside him and threw it after them. Bedwyr caught the dart in his hand and flung it back, and it pierced Yspaddaden Penkawr in the knee so that he cried out. "A cursed ungentlemanly son-in-law indeed!" he cried. "This dart pains me like the bite of

a gadfly. I shall ever walk the worse for his rudeness, and I shall never find a cure."

The knights went back to Custennin's house where they spent the night, returning at dawn the next day to the castle. Again they found Yspaddaden Penkawr in the hall, and again they asked of him his daughter in marriage, adding that there should be a handsome dowry which they would pay, both to her father and to her two kinswomen, and that if he refused he should be put to death.

"The maiden's four great-grandmothers and her four great-grandfathers are still alive," answered Yspaddaden Penkawr. "I must ask their advice before I give you my answer."

The knights agreed to this, and turned to leave him; but as they went he took up the second poisoned dart and threw it after them. But it did them no harm, for Menw caught the dart and flung it back, wounding Yspaddaden in the centre of the breast so that it pierced his body and came out of his back.

"A cursed ungentlemanly son-in-law indeed," he shouted. "This dart wounds me like the bite of a horse-leech. I shall feel it all my life."

The rest of the day the knights spent with Custennin and returned once more to the castle on the third day.

"Do not shoot at me again unless you wish to die," said Yspaddaden Penkawr as they came before him, and as he spoke he picked up the third poisoned dart and flung it at them. This time Kilhwch caught it and hurled it back, striking Yspaddaden in the eye.

"A cursed ungentlemanly son-in-law indeed," cried Yspaddaden Penkawr again. "The stroke of this dart is like the bite of a mad dog," and as the knights left they heard him cursing the fire in which the dart was forged.

The fourth day they came yet again, and Kilhwch was the first to speak.

"Do not shoot at us any more," he said, "unless you wish for even greater harm to come to yourself. Give me your daughter, for if you do not then you shall die."

"Come close, that I may see you!" said Yspaddaden, and a chair was placed for Kilhwch so that the two sat face to face. "I must have your pledge that you will treat me fairly, and then, when I have got what I shall ask of you, my daughter shall be yours."

"That I promise willingly," said Kilhwch. "Tell me what it is you wish me to do."

"You see yonder great hill," began Yspaddaden Penkawr. "I desire that it shall be rooted up and that it be ploughed and sewn in one day, and that in the same day the grain shall ripen, so that, of the wheat grown there, I can make food and drink for the wedding of you and my daughter. And all this must be done in one single day."

"It will be easy for me to do this," answered Kilhwch, "although you may not think so."

"If this is easy for you to do, there is something that will not be easy; for so wild is the land that no farmer can plough it except Amaethon the son of Don, and he will not come with you, and you will not be able to make him."

"That will be easy for me to do," said Kilhwch again, "even though you think it will not."

Then Yspaddaden asked of him thirty-six more tasks, and each one seemed impossible that it should ever be done. And every time a new problem was named Kilhwch answered in the same way, saying that the task was easy for him, even if Yspaddaden Penkawr did not think that it could be.

The last of the tasks that Yspaddaden demanded was that Kilhwch should bring the sword of Gwrnach the Giant. "He can never be slain except with his own sword, and he will not part with it either for gold or as a gift, and you will not be able to make him."

"My lord and kinsman Arthur will obtain all these things for me," answered Kilhwch, "and I shall win your daughter, and you shall lose your life," and he and the knights that were with him left the castle of Yspaddaden Penkawr.

That day they travelled far, and by evening they came to a great castle which was the largest in the world. And as they looked a black man, more than three times as big as any man they had ever seen, came out of the castle, and they stopped him and spoke to him.

"Whose is this castle?"

"You must be very stupid to ask a question like that," said the man. "Everyone in the world knows that it is the home of Gwrnach the Giant."

"Are guests welcome at the castle?"

"May Heaven protect you!" replied the man. "No guest has ever come out of there alive, and no one may enter unless he is a skilled craftsman and brings with him his craft."

The knights then rode to the gate and asked admittance of the porter, who refused to let them in, saying that the Giant was at his dinner, and the gate would not be opened that night except to a skilled craftsman.

"I am a craftsman," said Kai, "the best burnisher of swords in the whole world."

The porter took this message to Gwrnach, who said: "If he is skilled in the burnishing of swords, then we have need of him. For some time I have sought for someone to polish my sword, and could find none who could do it. Let this man come in!"

So Kai went in by himself and saluted the Giant, and a chair was placed for him beside Gwrnach, who asked him: "Is it true that you know how to burnish swords?" Kai said that it was indeed true, and when the sword was brought to him he took a whetstone and asked the Giant whether he would like it burnished white or blue.

"Do as it seems best to you, as if it were your own," was the

answer, and Kai polished half of the blade and gave it back to the Giant, saying: "Does this please you?"

Gwrnach was overjoyed. "I would rather the whole of the sword shone as does the part you have polished than anything else in the world. It is surprising to me that such a skilled workman should be without a companion."

"Oh noble sir," said Kai, "I have a companion, but he is not skilled in this art! He is outside, and his name is Bedwyr. Let your porter fetch him, and this is how he may recognize him. The head of my friend's lance will leave its shaft and draw blood from the wind, then return to the shaft again. He is very skilful, but he knows not this art."

Bedwyr was then brought into the castle, and with him came Custennin's son of the golden hair, whom they named Goreu, and Kai finished polishing the sword and gave it back to the Giant.

"The work is good," said Gwrnach. "I am pleased with it."

"It is the scabbard that is faulty and has made the sword rust. Give it to me that I may take out the wooden lining and put in a new one," and Kai picked up the sword in one hand and the scabbard in the other and, taking the Giant by surprise, he cut off his head with one blow. In the confusion that followed, the other knights broke into the castle which they sacked, taking from it what goods and jewels they could carry, and they returned to the Court of King Arthur, bearing with them the sword of Gwrnach the Giant.

When Arthur had finished listening to all that had happened to them, he considered which quest it would be best for them to tackle next, and decided that they should seek Mabon the son of Modron, the great huntsman whom Yspaddaden had demanded should be found. He had been stolen from his mother when only three days old, and now none knew whether he lived or was dead.

"First we must find his kinsman Eidoel, who is imprisoned in the Castle of Glivi," said Arthur, and he himself set out at the head of his warriors.

Glivi saw them coming from afar, and called out to know what it was that he could give them. "For I am ruined. Nothing remains to me, neither food nor joy, save this castle itself." He willingly agreed to give up his prisoner to show his friendship towards Arthur; so Eidoel joined them.

Then Arthur's followers begged the King to go home and not waste his time on such easy tasks. This Arthur agreed to do, and, picking out the same knights as before, bade them journey on with Kilhwch and Eidoel in search for Mabon.

They travelled on until they came to the Ousel, the wise bird of Cilgwri. Then Gwrhyr, who could speak all languages both of humans and of beasts, asked her if she could tell them anything of Mabon.

"When I first came here," answered the Ousel, "there was a smith's anvil in this place, and I was a young bird. Ever since then no work has been done upon it except for the pecking of my beak every evening, and this has worn it away to the size of a nut; yet in all this time I have never heard the name of Mabon spoken of. But I must do what I can to help an embassy from Arthur, so I will take you to a race of animals who are even older than I am," and she led the party to the Stag of Redynvre.

"Oh Stag of Redynvre," said Gwrhyr, "we are an embassy come from Arthur to seek your help, for you are the oldest animal we know. Can you tell us anything of Mabon son of Modron?"

"When I first came here," answered the Stag, "it was an open plain with but one tree, a sapling oak. I watched it grow into a fine oak with a hundred branches, and now it has died and nothing is there but its stump, yet I have never heard of this man. Nevertheless as you come from Arthur I will give you what help I can, and will show you where to find an animal who is older even than I."

He led them to the home of the Owl of Cwm Cawlwyd, and once again Gwrhyr asked for news of Mabon.

"If I knew I would tell you," said the Owl. "When I first came here the wide valley which you see was a wooded glen. Men came and rooted it up, and a second wood grew in its place, and the wood you now see is the third. Yet until you spoke it yourself I have never heard the name mentioned. But I will willingly lead Arthur's embassy to the oldest animal in the world and the one who has travelled most, the Eagle of Gwern Abwy."

The Eagle was ready to help them. He said: "When I first came here there was a great rock, from the top of which I pecked at the stars every evening; but now it is not so much as a span high. In all that time I have only once heard the name spoken, and that was when I went in search of food as far as Llyn Llyw. There I saw a salmon, and quickly stuck my talons into him; but he drew me into deep water and I barely escaped with my life. So I gathered my kindred together and went to attack him; but he sent messages of peace, and coming to the surface begged me to take fifty fish spears out of his back. I can think of no one else who might be able to help you, and I will lead you to him."

This he did, and called upon the salmon for help.

"I will tell you as much as I know," said the salmon. "With every tide I go up the river as far as the walls of Gloucester, and there I have found such wickedness as I never saw before. That you may believe me, will two of you come with me, one upon each of my shoulders?"

So Kai and Gwrhyr rode on the shoulders of the salmon until they came to the walls of Gloucester Castle, and there they heard sounds of great wailing and sorrow coming from the dungeon.

"Who is it that cries out in that dungeon?" asked Gwrhyr.

"It is Mabon the son of Modron, and dreadful is his lot."

"Can his release be bought by gold or silver, or can he be set free by fighting?"

"Only by fighting," was the answer.

So the knights returned quickly to King Arthur, who came to Gloucester with his warriors and attacked the castle. And while they fought in the front of the castle Kai and Gwrhyr broke through the walls of the dungeon and rescued Mabon, and they took him back with them to Arthur's Court.

King Arthur made Mabon welcome; then, without loss of time, he and his warriors continued to solve the problems which had been put before them. At last, after much skilful thought and fierce fighting, all were done. Then Kilhwch and Goreu, the son of the herdsman Custennin, and many others, taking with them Mabon the son of Modron, the sword of Gwrnach the Giant and every trophy that had been demanded of them, returned to the castle of Yspaddaden Penkawr and laid all before him.

"Is thy daughter mine now?" asked Kilhwch.

"She is thine. But thank not me but Arthur, who has done this thing for you. Never would I have given her to you, for with her I lose my life."

Then Goreu seized him by his hair and dragged him to the keep. There Goreu cut off his head and placed it on a stake on the citadel, and they took possession of the castle with all its treasures. And that night Olwen became Kilhwch's bride, and she continued to be his wife as long as she lived.

The Lady of the Fountain

ONE day, when King Arthur was at his chief palace at Caerlleon, he said to his knights: "If you will not think me idle I should like to sleep while I wait for my meal, and you can entertain each other by relating tales, while Kai will give you meat and drink," and with that he went to sleep on his couch of green rushes spread with a cloth of red satin.

Then Kynon, who was one of Arthur's knights, asked Kai for the food which the King had promised them; so Kai went to the kitchen and the cellars and brought back a flagon of mead with a golden goblet, and a handful of skewers, on each of which was a slice of meat.

"Here is your food," said Kai, "and now that I have given it to you you must repay me by telling a story."

With a little hesitation Kynon was persuaded to do this.

"I was an only son," he began, "and so ambitious that there were not adventures enough in my own country to keep me happy. I thought that there was no task too great for me to be able to do, and taking a horse and armour I set out to find my fortune.

"At last I came to the fairest valley in the world, with trees of equal height and a path running along by a river, which I followed. At the end of the valley I came to a plain in which stood a handsome castle. Riding towards it I saw two youths with yellow curling hair, each dressed in yellow satin and wearing a golden circlet on his head. Each carried an ivory bow, and their arrows had shafts of whalebone tipped with gold and were winged with peacocks' feathers: their daggers, which they were shooting, had blades of gold and hilts of whalebone.

"Not far off stood a man in the prime of life with his beard newly cut, dressed in a robe of yellow satin, round the top of which was a band of gold lace, and his shoes were fastened by studs of gold. I gave him greetings, which he returned with great courtesy, and he led me on towards the castle, which appeared to be empty except for one room, in the window of which sat twenty-four maidens embroidering on satin. And I can tell you, Kai, that the least of these was fairer than any maid in the Island of Britain, even our Queen Gwenhwyvar when she is at her most beautiful.

"These maidens got up when we went in, and six of them took my horse and unharnessed him as well as if they had been the best squires in the land. Six others took my arms and washed them till they shone: six more spread the table and prepared the dinner; while the fourth six took off my soiled garments and gave me fresh, with a yellow satin mantle trimmed with a broad gold band. They brought me red linen cushions and silver bowls of water in which I could wash.

"In a little while the man sat down at the table, which was of silver and laid with dishes all of silver or gold. I sat beside him, and below me were the maidens, except for those who waited upon us: and truly, Kai, the meal was better served than I have seen anywhere else. Until dinner was over, no one spoke; then the man asked me who I was, and I told him how glad I was that he had spoken, for I had been afraid that it was the rule of the castle that there should be no talking.

" 'I would have spoken sooner,' said the man, 'but I feared to disturb you while you ate.' So I told him who I was and that I was travelling to find out whether anyone was greater than I in battle, or if I could win the mastery over all.

"Then the man smiled and said that, if it would not distress me too much, he could show me the answer to my question.

" 'Sleep here tonight,' he said, 'then tomorrow morning early take the road by which you came until you reach the wood at the top of the valley, then turn down the road to the right and go on until you come to a large, sheltered glade with a mound in the centre. On the top of this mound you will see an enormous black man, larger than two ordinary men. He is extremely ugly, and he has only one foot, and one eye which is in the middle of his forehead, and he carries a club so heavy that no two men could lift it. He is the Keeper of the Wood, and a thousand wild animals graze round him. Ask him to show you the way out of the glade, and he will point out the road by which you will find the answer to that which you seek.'

"The next morning I rose early, and followed the directions I had been given until I came to the glade. There I was three times more astonished at the number of animals gathered together than the man had said I should be. And when I saw the black man he was larger by far than I had expected, and as for his club, I am certain, Kai, that even four warriors could not lift it.

"He answered my questions, but said nothing more, and when I asked him what power he had over the animals he said: 'I will show you.' At that he struck the stag with his club and the stag brayed loudly. At the sound of his braying all the animals came towards the mound, serpents, dragons and every kind of creature crowding so thickly together that I could hardly find room to stand. Then the black man looked at them with his one eye and they bowed their heads as though they were vassals before their lord, and he told them to go and feed.

"Then the black man said to me: 'You see, little man, what power I have over these animals,' but when I asked him the way he became very rude and rough. However when I told him who I was and what I wanted he said:

" 'Go to the end of the glade and climb the steep hill through the wood till you come to the top. There you will find an open space with a tall tree in the middle of it, the branches of which are greener than the greenest pine-trees. Under this tree is a fountain with a marble slab beside it on which is a silver bowl attached to

it by a chain of silver. Take the bowl and throw a bowlful of water
upon the slab. Then there will come a mighty peal of thunder
so loud as to seem as though heaven and earth were trembling
with fury, and with the thunder a hailstorm so severe that you
will scarcely live through it. After the shower the weather will
become fine, but every leaf on the tree will have been swept away
by the storm. Next a flight of birds will settle in the tree, and they
will sing a song sweeter than any you have ever heard in your
own country. But at the moment when it is most delighting
you a murmuring, complaining sound will come to you from the
valley, and you will see a knight upon a coal-black horse, dressed
in black velvet and with a black flag on his lance riding towards
you. He will rush to attack you with the greatest speed. If you
flee from him, he will catch you, and if you stay and fight as sure
as you are a mounted knight I tell you he will leave you on foot.
And if you don't find trouble in that adventure you need seek it
no more for the rest of your life.'

"So I went on till I found the tree, and everything happened
just as the black man had said, though I found the thunder more
violent even than he had described, and I assure you, Kai, that
the storm was such that neither man nor beast could live in it.
I turned my horse's head towards the hail and held the point of
my shield over his head and neck and the upper part over my
own, and thus escaped the worst. When I looked at the tree there
was not a single leaf on it. When the birds came their song was so
sweet that I have never heard any melody equal to it before or
since. When I was most charmed by it a voice called to me out of
the valley, saying: 'Oh knight, what has brought you here, and
what evil have I done you that you should act towards me and
my country as you have today? Do you not know that the storm
swept over my land, leaving no man nor beast that was exposed
to it alive?' Then the knight in black velvet rode up and we charged
each other furiously, but it was not long before I was overthrown.
Then, taking no notice of me, the knight passed the shaft of his

lance through my horse's bridle and rode off with the two horses, leaving me standing there alone.

"So there was nothing for me to do but to return the way I had come, and when I reached the glade where the black man was I confess to you, Kai, that his derision and laughter were almost more than I could stand. But when I got back to the castle I was made most welcome, and I was better entertained even than I had been the night before. Nobody mentioned my expedition to the fountain; but the next morning when I was about to leave I found ready saddled a dark bay horse with nostrils of scarlet, and after putting on my armour I left my blessings with those who had treated me so well and returned home. I still have that horse—you may see him in the stable here—and I would not part with him for the best palfrey in the Island of Britain.

"There is your story, Kai, and I am sure no man has ever confessed to an adventure so much to his discredit."

"Would it not be a good idea to try to discover that place?" said Owain; but Kai jeered at him and said that it was very fine to talk like that, but he would never really go upon such a venture.

The Queen rebuked him sternly for speaking to so valiant a knight as Owain in that way, and just then Arthur woke from his sleep, and it was time for dinner.

The next morning Owain armed himself and left the Court. After much travelling and searching through far distant lands he came at last to a valley, which he felt sure was the one that Kynon had described. He rode along it till he reached the castle in the plain, and all was as he had been told even to the two youths shooting their daggers, and the man dressed in yellow satin, who took him into the castle. When Owain saw the twenty-four maidens working at their embroidery, he thought that their beauty was even greater than Kynon had told him, and they waited on him and gave him dinner, and everything was of the best.

"I am in search of the knight who guards the Fountain," he

told the man who had brought him in, and again the man, smiling, said he liked telling him the way no more than he had liked telling Kynon; but since that was Owain's desire he would give him full directions.

The next morning Owain found that the maidens had saddled his horse, and he set out and soon came to the glade where he found the black Keeper of the Wood, whom he thought even larger than Kynon had described him. All went as before, and when Owain, reaching the green tree, threw the bowlful of water on the slab, the thunder and the hailstorm were even more violent than he had expected. When at last the birds settled on the leafless tree and he was enjoying their beautiful singing, he saw the knight in black coming to him through the valley, and made ready for battle.

They fought together violently, and when their lances were broken they fought with their swords. Then Owain struck the knight a mighty blow on his helmet which cut right through to his brain, and the knight, fearing that he had received his death wound, turned his horse's head and fled. Owain took up the pursuit and was close behind the knight when they came to a large and handsome castle. The knight rode in through the gate; but as Owain followed close on his heels the portcullis was dropped with a crash, striking Owain's horse just behind the saddle, cutting him in two and carrying away Owain's spurs. The inner gate before him was closed, but looking through an open panel in it he could see a street facing him with houses on either side. As he looked he saw a maiden with yellow curling hair with a band of gold upon her head, and she came up to the gate and asked that it should be opened.

"Lady," said Owain, "here I am with half a horse, and it is no more possible for me to open the gate for you than it is for you to set me free."

"It is very sad that you cannot be released," she said, "and every woman ought to help you, for I never knew anyone who does more to serve ladies than you do. You are our most sincere friend and devoted lover, and because of this I will do anything I can to help you." Then, taking a ring from her finger and passing it to him through the open panel, she said: "Wear this ring with the stone turned inwards and close your hand upon it. As long as you hide the stone it will hide you. When those in the castle have heard what has happened they will come to fetch you in order to kill you, and they will be very worried when they cannot find you. I will wait for you on the horse-block along the road, and you will be able to see me though I cannot see you; so when the gate is open come and put your hand on my shoulder and I will know that you are there. I shall then move away, and you must follow me."

She left the gate, and Owain put on the ring with the stone turned into his hand. Before long, as she had said, men came from the castle to put him to death, and they were amazed when all they found between the portcullis and the gate was half a horse. As Owain was now invisible it was easy for him to slip through the gate and find the maiden sitting on the horse-block. As soon as he touched her she rose, and he followed her until they came to the door of a beautiful room in which the walls were painted in gorgeous colours with an image of gold in every panel, while even the nails were coloured in the brightest shades.

The maiden lit a fire and brought him water for washing in a silver bowl. When he was ready she placed before him a silver table inlaid with gold and spread with a cloth of yellow linen, and she brought him a meal so excellent that he thought he had never tasted food that was better cooked nor wine so well chosen. All was served in dishes of gold and silver, and Owain feasted until late in the afternoon, when he was disturbed by a great clamour in the castle.

"What is the meaning of this noise?" he asked the maiden.

"They are holding the last service for the Nobleman who owns this castle."

Then the maiden led him to a rich scarlet couch of fur, satin and fine silk, and he went to sleep.

In the middle of the night he was woken by a sound of loud lamentations coming from the castle.

"What is the meaning of this outcry?" he asked the maiden.

"The Nobleman who owns this castle is now dead," she said, and when, a little after daybreak, they heard an even louder wailing in the castle, she told him that they were taking the Nobleman's body to the church.

Then Owain got up and dressed, and looking from the window he saw a vast crowd of men filling the streets. They were fully armed, and with them were many women both on horseback and on foot, and all the monks and priests in the city were singing so loudly that with the sound of the trumpets and the wailing of the crowd the noise seemed to fill the whole sky. In the middle of the crowd, covered in white linen and carried by men of high rank, he saw the bier with wax tapers burning beside it. Never had he beheld so magnificent a procession nor so much satin and fine silk. Following the train was a lady dressed in yellow satin, and her hair, which fell over her shoulders, was stained with blood. She beat her hands together with great violence, and her cry was louder than the shout of the men or the clamour of the trumpets. So beautiful was she that Owain no sooner saw her than he fell deeply in love, and he asked the maiden who this was.

"She is my mistress," said the maiden, "and she is said to be the fairest, the wisest and the most noble of women. She is called the Countess of the Fountain, and was the wife of the Nobleman that you killed yesterday."

"In truth," said Owain, "she is the lady I love best."

"In truth," said the maiden, "she shall come to love you too."

Then the maiden got up, lit a fire and placed a pot of water to warm. Then she tied a white linen towel round Owain's neck, and filling an ivory goblet and a silver basin with warm water, she washed Owain's head. After this, taking a razor with an ivory handle, she shaved his beard. This done she brought him food, and again Owain thought he had never had so good a meal nor one so well served.

As soon as he had finished the maiden led him back to his couch, saying: "Come and sleep, and I will go and woo for you," and leaving him she made her way towards the castle.

When she went inside she found nothing but mourning and sorrow. The Countess, who had retired to her own room, was so deeply distressed that she could not bear the sight of any living person, and when Luned, which was the maiden's name, went in, the Countess would have nothing to do with her. But the maiden knelt down beside her and begged her to speak.

"Luned," said the Countess, "what has happened that you did not come to me in my great grief? I have treated you well and given you riches; it was wrong of you that you did not come when I needed you most."

"I had thought you had more courage and good sense," answered Luned. "What is the good of longing for a man that is dead, or for anything else that you cannot have?"

"In the whole world there is no one to equal him," said the Countess sadly.

"That is not true," answered Luned, "for an ugly man would be as good or better than he was."

"If it were not that I have brought you up and treated you as my own daughter I would have you executed for saying such a thing. As it is, I will banish you."

"I am glad that I have done nothing worse to cause your anger than try to help you. You do not know what is for your own good, and ill betide whichever of us tries first to make friends with the other after this," said Luned and went quickly from the room.

But the Countess got up and moved to the door. She stood there a moment, then coughed loudly. Luned looked round, and when she saw the Countess beckoning,she went back into the room.

"You have behaved spitefully," said the Countess, "but if you know something to my advantage will you tell me what it is?"

"I do indeed," said Luned. "You know well that except by force you will not be able to guard your possessions. I therefore beg you to find someone who will protect you and all that is yours without delay."

"How can I do that?"

"I will tell you," answered Luned. "Unless you defend the Fountain you will not be able to keep your lands, and no one can do that except one of King Arthur's knights. I will travel to Arthur's Court, and it will go ill with me if I do not bring back to you a warrior who can guard the Fountain as well as if not better than he who defended it before."

"That is a hard task," said the Countess, "but go, and see if you can make good your promise."

So Luned set out, pretending to go to the Court of King Arthur, but instead she went to the room where Owain lay, and she stayed there with him as long as it would have taken her to go to Arthur's Court and back. When she thought the right time had come she dressed herself in travelling clothes and went to the Countess, who was very pleased to see her and asked what was the result of her visit.

"I bring the best of news," said Luned, "for I have succeeded in my quest. When may I present to you the knight who has come back with me?"

"Bring him at midday tomorrow," said the Countess, "and I will call the townsfolk together at that time."

The next day Luned dressed Owain in a yellow satin mantle on which was a broad band of gold. On his feet he wore high shoes of coloured leather fastened by gold clasps in the form of lions, and they went together to the Countess.

The Countess welcomed them gladly, but she looked hard at Owain and said: "This knight does not look as if he had travelled far."

"What does that matter?" asked Luned.

"I am certain that this is the man who killed my husband."

"So much the better," said Luned. "For if he had not been stronger than your lord he could not have got the better of him. What is past is past, and there is no help for it."

"Go back to your house," said the Countess, "and I will take the advice of my counsellors."

The next day the Countess called all her subjects together and showed them that her earldom was left unprotected, and that it could not be defended except by great military skill. "Therefore," she said, "I give you your choice. Either let one of you come forward to be my lord and defend my lands, or else give your consent for me to seek a protector elsewhere."

After some discussion they decided that it would be better that the Countess should have their permission to marry someone from outside her dominions if he would undertake to protect them all, so she sent for the bishops and archbishops to arrange for her marriage with Owain, and all the men of her lands did homage to Owain.

From then on Owain defended the Fountain. Every knight that came to it he overthrew and sold him for his full worth, and the money he obtained he divided among his barons and knights, and he was much beloved by his people, and so it went on for three years.

Meanwhile at home at his Court Arthur grew very sad. Gwalchmai was much troubled at this, and one day he determined to ask Arthur the cause of his sorrow.

"Indeed, Gwalchmai," said Arthur, "I am grieving at the loss of Owain. I have not seen him for three years, and I shall certainly die if a fourth passes and he does not come back. I am sure that it is because of the tale Kynon told that he has gone away, and I intend to go in search of him."

"There is no need for you to call out the army," said Gwalchmai, "for you yourself and the knights of your Court will be able to avenge Owain if he has been killed, or to set him free if he is imprisoned; while if he is alive you can bring him back with you."

This seemed to Arthur a wise suggestion, and he called together the knights of his household, which numbered three thousand, and together with their attendants set out in search of Owain, taking Kynon as their guide.

When at last they came to the castle the two youths were shooting in the same place, and beside them stood the man dressed in a robe of yellow satin just as Kynon had described. This man gave them greeting and invited Arthur and his host to come inside, and so great was the size of the castle that their vast number was hardly noticeable. As before, the maidens came to wait upon them, and even King Arthur had never met with such excellent service. The very page in charge of the horses was as well looked after as Arthur himself in his own castle.

The next morning Kynon led them to the glade where the one-eyed Keeper of the Wood was to be found, and the black man seemed so huge that even after Kynon's description Arthur was amazed. When they reached the green tree and saw the slab and bowl beside the fountain Kai went to Arthur and asked that he might be the one to throw the bowl of water upon the slab.

As soon as he had done so there was a mighty clap of thunder followed by a storm of hail so violent that many who were in Arthur's train were killed. When it cleared, the birds came and perched on the now leafless tree, and their song was more beautiful than any the King and his men had ever heard. While they were listening a knight clad in black satin and riding a coal-black horse came rushing towards them and attacked Kai, who was soon thrown from his horse. Then the knight rode away, and Arthur and his host encamped for the night.

The next morning the knight came again, and Kai went to Arthur and asked his permission to do battle once more. Arthur gave him leave, and Kai and the knight fought, and again Kai was overthrown, this time with a bad wound in his head, so that he could not go on with the battle. After that all Arthur's warriors fought in turn with the knight, who unhorsed them every one till only Arthur himself and Gwalchmai were left.

Then Arthur armed himself and prepared for the encounter; but Gwalchmai begged that he might be allowed to meet the knight first. Arthur agreed, and, wearing a satin robe of honour over his armour in which he could not be recognized, Gwalchmai went forward to meet the knight. All that day they fought until evening came, and neither was able to unhorse the other. The next day they went on with the battle, but still neither could gain the mastery. On the third day they fought with great fury until noon, when they charged each other with such violence that the girths broke on their horses and they both fell to the ground. Leaping to their feet, the two knights drew their swords and went on fighting, and the crowd watching them thought that never had there been so valiant a battle as the sparks flew from their swords and lighted up the whole scene. Then the knight gave Gwalchmai such a blow that it broke his helmet from his face, and the knight could see whom it was that he fought.

Dropping his sword he cried: "My lord Gwalchmai, I did not know that it was you, my own cousin, because of the robe you are wearing. Take my sword and my arms, for you are the victor," and he uncovered his face, and all saw that it was Owain who fought.

"Not so," answered Gwalchmai, "for you are the victor, and I beg that you will take my sword."

When Arthur saw that they had stopped fighting and were talking to each other he came forward.

"My lord Arthur," cried Gwalchmai, "here is Owain. He has conquered me and will not take my sword."

"Not so," said Owain. "It is he that has vanquished me, and he will not take my sword."

"Give me your swords," commanded Arthur, "for neither of you has conquered the other."

Then Owain embraced Arthur, and the host hurried forward to greet Owain in a great rush.

That night they spent in the camp, and the next day Arthur prepared to leave for home.

"My lord," begged Owain, "this you must not do. I have been away from you for three years, and all that time I have been preparing a banquet for you, knowing that you would come to seek for me. Stay with me, I beg you, till you and your attendants have rested from the toils of the journey."

Then they all went on to the castle of the Countess of the Fountain, and the banquet which had taken three years to prepare was eaten in three months, and never had a feast been more enjoyed.

When Arthur at last prepared to leave for home he sent a message to the Countess begging her to let Owain go back with him for three months that his friends in the Island of Britain might see him again, and the Countess agreed though it made her very sad. So Owain returned with them, and when he reached the Court of King Arthur he stayed there three years instead of three months.

Owain and the Lion

ONE day when Owain sat at dinner in the city of Caerlleon a maiden dressed in yellow satin came riding in upon a bay horse covered with foam, which had a curling mane and a bridle and saddle of gold. She came up to Owain and took a ring from his hand, saying: "Thus shall be treated the deceiver, the traitor, the faithless and the disgraced," and, turning her horse, she rode away.

Then Owain, remembering the adventure of which she spoke, was very sorrowful, and the next day he left the Court of King Arthur and wandered away to far distant parts of the earth and rugged, uninhabited mountains. There he stayed until his clothes were worn out and his hair grown long, while he himself was wasted away with hunger and sorrow. He lived with the wild beasts and fed with them until they grew to know him and accepted him as one of themselves; but at last he grew so weak that he could no longer go about with them. Then he left the mountains and came down to a valley in which he saw a park, the finest in the world, belonging to a Countess who was a widow.

One day the Countess was walking in the park with her maidens and she saw Owain lying on the ground. The maidens were very much afraid, but they went up and one of them, touching him, saw that he was still alive. Then the Countess returned to the castle and, taking a flask full of precious ointment, gave it to one of the maidens, saying: "Take this balsam and anoint the man we saw just now with it, and if he is still alive he will recover and get up. Take also a horse and clothing and put them near him, and watch what he will do."

So the maiden went back to the park and poured the whole contents of the flask over Owain, left the horse and clothing near to him, and hid in the bushes to watch.

In a short time Owain began to move his arms, then, still very weak, he got up and, looking at his ragged garments, felt greatly shamed. Then he saw the horse with the clothing on its saddle, and, creeping forward, he was able to draw the garments to him and put them on, and with great difficulty mounted the horse. As soon as he was in the saddle the maiden came forward, and Owain, overcome with joy at seeing a human person again, asked her where he was and on whose land.

"A widowed Countess owns the castle which you can see," said the maiden. "When her husband died he left her two Earldoms; but now she has only this one castle, for all the rest of her lands have been stolen from her by her neighbour, a young Earl, because she will not marry him." Then she took him back to the castle and led him to a pleasant room, where she lit a fire and left him to rest.

Then she returned to the Countess and gave her back the flask. When the Countess saw that it was empty she was very much upset.

"Where is the balsam?" she asked.

"I have used it all," answered the maiden.

"That I cannot easily forgive you," said the Countess, "for you have wasted a hundred and forty pounds worth of precious ointment upon a stranger. However you had better look after him until he has recovered."

So the maiden went back to Owain and saw that he had food and comfortable lodgings and all the medicines that he needed to make him well again, and in three months he was restored to health and was even more handsome than he had been before.

One day while resting he heard a great uproar and noise of clashing arms in the castle, and he asked the maiden what was happening.

"The young Earl of whom I told you has come to the castle with a great army to take the Countess."

Then Owain asked her if the Countess had a horse and arms in the castle.

"She has the best in the world," answered the maiden, and Owain urged her to go to the Countess and beg the loan of armour and a horse for him that he might ride out to see the army.

When she delivered his message the Countess laughed and said: "I will give him a horse and arms to keep for himself, and I am sure he has never seen such good ones, and I am glad that he will have them, for tomorrow my enemies will take them from me; though I cannot think what he means to do with them." Then she ordered her groom to bring out a beautiful black charger with armour for both horse and man, and Owain armed himself and went out, attended by two pages.

When he came near the Earl's army so vast was it that it stretched away into the distance on every side and he could not see its full extent, and he asked the pages in which troop the Earl himself was to be found.

"He is over there," said the pages, "where you can see four yellow standards: two are before him and two behind."

Then Owain told them to go back to the castle and wait for him near the gate, and he rode forward to meet the Earl. A fierce battle ensued, and Owain overthrew the Earl, turned his horse, and with great difficulty managed to lead him back to the gate where the pages were waiting. They took him into the castle, and Owain presented the Earl as a gift to the Countess, saying: "Here is a return to you for your blessed gift of balsam."

As a ransom for his life the young Earl restored to the Countess all that he had taken from her, and for his freedom he gave her half of his own lands and all his gold and silver and jewels as well as hostages.

The Countess was overjoyed and begged Owain to remain at the castle with her; but he refused, and once more set out on his travels in distant lands.

One day as he was passing a wood he heard a loud yelling coming from within it, and, hurrying towards the sound, he found a huge craggy mound in the middle of the wood on the side of which was a grey rock. In a cleft of the rock was a serpent and nearby a black lion, and every time the lion tried to escape, the serpent shot forward and attacked him. Then Owain went up to the rock, and as the serpent darted out he struck it with his sword and cut it in two; then, drying his sword, he continued on his way. At this the lion followed him and played about round his horse as though it had been a greyhound which he had trained.

In this way they went forward till evening, when Owain dismounted and turned his horse loose in a wooded meadow. He made himself a fire, and, when it was burning, the lion brought him fuel enough to last for three nights, and then went off. It soon returned, bringing with it a large roebuck which it had caught, and flung it down beside Owain.

Then Owain skinned the roebuck and cut it up, placing slices of the meat on skewers round the fire for his meal, and giving the rest to the lion to eat. While he was doing this he heard a deep sigh near to him, and then another sigh, and a third. Seeing no one,

Owain called out to know if it was a human being that was near him, and, hearing that it was, he said: "Who are you?"

"I am Luned, the servant of the Countess of the Fountain."

"What are you doing here?" asked Owain.

"I am imprisoned," replied the voice, "because of the knight who came from Arthur's Court and married the Countess. He stayed a short time with her, then returned to King Arthur and has not been back since, and he was the friend I loved best in the world. And two of the pages lied about him and called him a deceiver, and I told them that the two of them together were not worth one of him; so they imprisoned me in this stone vault, and said that unless the knight came himself to deliver me by a certain day I should be put to death. And the day they named is only two days away, and I have no one to send to seek him for me, and his name is Owain son of Urien."

"Are you sure that if the knight knew all this he would come to your rescue?" asked Owain.

"I am certain of it."

When the meat was cooked, Owain divided it between himself and the maiden, passing her share in to her in the stone cell, and after they had eaten they talked together till morning, and the lion kept watch over them through the night.

When the dawn came Owain asked the maiden if there was anywhere near where he could get food and rest.

"There is indeed," said Luned. "If you follow the river you will soon come to a great castle with many towers, and the Earl who owns it is the most hospitable man in the world. He will make you welcome, and there you can spend the night."

Owain found that it was just as she had said, and he was made welcome and his horse well cared for, and the lion went to the manger and lay down beside his horse so that nobody dared to come near. But it seemed to Owain that some tragedy lay over the castle, for everyone he met appeared to be weighed down with sorrow. When they went in to dinner Owain sat by the Earl with the Earl's daughter, who was very beautiful, on his other side. The lion came and lay between Owain's feet, and Owain fed him with portions of all the food he himself was given.

In the middle of dinner the Earl again said how glad he was to see his guest, so Owain answered him: "In that case is it not time for you to be more cheerful?"

"Indeed it is not your coming that makes us sorrowful," said the Earl, "but we have much cause for sadness. I have two sons, and yesterday they went to the mountains to hunt. Now there is on the mountain a monster in the form of a gigantic man who kills and eats men, and he seized both my sons, and tomorrow he says that he will come here, and he will kill my sons before my eyes unless I will give him my daughter in marriage."

"That is indeed terrible," said Owain. "Which will you do?"

"It would be better that my sons should be killed than that I should willingly give my daughter to such a creature," answered the Earl; then they talked of other matters, and Owain stayed the night at the castle.

The next morning he heard the giant arrive with much shouting and clamour, bringing the two youths, and the Earl was sorely tried in his endeavour both to protect his castle and save his sons. Then Owain put on his armour and went out to meet the giant, and the lion followed him. When the giant saw that Owain was armed he rushed to the attack, and violent was the battle between them; and the lion joined in and fought even more furiously than Owain.

"I should find no difficulty in fighting this man," cried out the giant, "if it were not for the animal with him."

Hearing this, Owain took the lion and shut him up in the castle, then returned to fight the giant. But Owain had not regained his full strength, and when the lion heard that things were not going well with him it roared loudly and climbed up to the top of the hall and from thence to the top of the castle, and it sprang down from the walls and again took part in the fight. Then the

lion gave the giant a mighty stroke which tore him open from the shoulder to the hip, and the giant fell down dead, and Owain restored the two boys to their father.

The Earl was filled with joy and begged that Owain would remain with him; but Owain refused and set out for the meadow where he had found Luned. As he drew near he saw a great fire burning and two youths with curling auburn hair leading the maiden towards it that they might cast her into the flames. Owain called to them to stop, and asked them what charge they had against the maiden, and they told him of the bargain they had made with her.

"And," they said, "Owain has failed her, so we are taking her to be burnt."

"But he is a good knight," said Owain, "and if he knew that the maiden was in such peril I am amazed that he did not come to her rescue; but if you will accept me in place of him I will do battle with you."

To this the youths agreed, and quickly rushed to attack him, and they fought so well that Owain was hard pressed. Seeing this, the lion came to his help, and the two of them soon defeated the two young men.

"Lord," cried one of the youths, "it was agreed that we should fight with you alone, and not with that animal as well."

At that Owain took the lion to the cell where Luned had been imprisoned and shut it in, blocking up the door with stones, then went back to fight the two young men alone. But, being still weak from his illness, he was hardly able to keep them at bay. When the lion saw that Owain was in trouble it roared continuously, and at last burst through the wall of stones, rushed on the young men and instantly killed them.

Thus Luned was saved from the fire, and Owain took her back to the castle of the Countess of the Fountain. He then persuaded the Countess to go with him to the Court of King Arthur, and she was his wife as long as she lived.

Peredur the Son of Evrawc

THE Earl Evrawc was a knight of great renown. He had seven sons, and he spent his time fighting, both in tournaments and in wars. In this way he was slain, and so were his six elder sons. The youngest, Peredur, was still too young to fight when his father died, and his mother was determined that he should not meet with the same fate.

This thought worried her so much that she took Peredur from his home and went to live in the desert where nobody dwelt, and let only women, young boys and men of a peaceful nature go with them: nor would she allow any riding-horses or arms of war to be taken in case her son should become interested in these things. Here it was that Peredur grew up, and he spent much of his time in the forest practising the art of throwing sticks.

One day when he was doing this he saw his mother's herd of goats, and near them stood two hinds which, he was surprised to see, had no horns. Being very quick and active, he was able to drive them into the shed where the goats were kept at the end of the forest; then he hurried back to his mother.

"I have seen such a marvellous thing," he told her. "Two of your goats have run wild and lost their horns through being so long in the woods. I had great trouble in getting them back to the shed."

A few days later three knights, who came from King Arthur's Court, rode up the fairway on the edge of the forest: Gwalchmai, Arthur's nephew, with Geneir Gwystyl and Owain.

"Mother," cried Peredur, "what are those?"

"They are angels, my son," she answered.

"Then I will go and be an angel with them," said Peredur, and he hurried to meet them.

As he came up Owain called out: "Have you seen a knight pass this way, either today or yesterday?"

"I don't know what a knight is."

"Someone like me," answered Owain.

"If you will tell me what I want to know I will answer your question," said Peredur.

"I will gladly tell you what you ask."

"What is this?" asked Peredur, touching his saddle.

"It is a saddle," said Owain, and then, in reply to Peredur's questions, he told him about his horse, his arms and the use to which each one was put.

Then Peredur, who had listened eagerly to all that he had been told, said: "Go forward, for I saw him whom you described pass this way, and I will follow you."

Peredur then went back to his mother and told her: "These are not angels, but honourable knights," which so filled her with fear that she fainted right away. But Peredur went to the stables where the pack-horses were kept and chose from among them a bony piebald horse which he thought was the strongest there. Then he pressed down a pack into the shape of a saddle, and took twigs and twisted them to look like the trappings that were on the knight's horse. This done he went back to his mother, who had recovered from the shock of knowing that he had discovered what she had so long kept hidden from him, and she asked him if he wished to ride away.

"Yes, with your permission."

"Go, then, to the Court of King Arthur," said his mother, "where you will find the best and the most valiant of men. And whenever you see a church, stop and speak your Paternoster to it. If you are hungry and you see meat and drink and nobody offers it to you, then help yourself to what you need, and if you should hear a cry for help, especially if it is made by a woman, then go quickly towards it. If you see a handsome jewel, take it and give it to someone else; for in that way you will gain praise, and if you see a beautiful woman then pay court to her, for in so doing you will make yourself a better man than you were before." So Peredur said goodbye to his mother, mounted his horse and, taking with him a handful of sharp-pointed forks, he rode away.

For two days and two nights he travelled through the country-side without anything to eat or drink until at last he came to a glade in a wild wood. Here he saw a tent and, thinking it to be a church, Peredur said his Paternoster to it. But as he drew nearer he saw a lovely auburn-haired maiden with a large gold ring on her hand sitting on a golden chair near the door of the tent, and she made him welcome.

"My mother told me whenever I saw food and drink to take it," said Peredur looking at the two flasks of wine and the bread and meat inside the tent door.

"Take the meat willingly," answered the maiden, and Peredur took half of what was there and left the rest for her. Then, kneeling on one knee before her, he said: "My mother told me whenever I saw a fine jewel I was to take it."

"Do so, my friend," replied the maiden, and he took her ring, mounted his horse and went on his way.

Before long the Lord of the Glade, to whom the tent belonged, returned, and, seeing the track of a horse, he asked who had been there while he was away.

"Did he harm or insult you?" asked the knight.

"No, indeed, he harmed me not."

But this the knight would not believe. He grew very angry and swore that he would follow Peredur and avenge both his lady and himself. "And until I have found him you shall not remain two nights in the same house," he said, and taking her with him he set out to find Peredur.

Meanwhile Peredur rode on towards the Court of King Arthur. He reached it at last and was about to enter when another knight came up ahead of him, gave the porter a ring of thick gold for holding his horse and went into the hall where Arthur sat with his wife Gwenhwyvar and their courtiers, just at the moment when a page was handing Gwenhwyvar a golden goblet of wine. The knight stepped suddenly forward, seized the goblet and flung the wine into the Queen's face and down her dress, then gave her a violent blow on the face.

"If any knight here has the courage to avenge his Queen for this insult, let him follow me to the meadow," he cried, "and there I will await him," and, taking his horse, he rode off to the meadow.

At this there was great fear among the knights of the Court; for they felt that no one could behave in such a manner unless he was protected by sorcery and strong charms against which none of them could hope to win in a fair fight.

It was at this moment that Peredur rode into the Court on his bony piebald horse with its strange trappings of twisted wood, and he came up to Kai, a knight of the Court, who stood in the centre of the hall.

"Tell me, tall man," demanded Peredur, "is that indeed King Arthur?"

"What do you want from Arthur?" asked Kai.

"My mother told me to go to him and receive the honour of knighthood."

"You are no knight," said Kai. "You have no arms nor trappings nor a worthy horse," and the rest of the Court looked up and began throwing sticks at him. Then up came a dwarf with his dwarfess wife who had been at the Court for a year and had never spoken a word. But when the dwarf saw Peredur he said: "Welcome, good Peredur son of Evrawc, the chief of warriors, the flower of knighthood."

This made Kai very angry. "For a year you have not spoken," he said, "and now you dare to call a poor man like this the flower of knighthood," and he hit the dwarf so hard that he fell to the ground senseless.

At this the dwarfess welcomed Peredur with the same words,

and Kai kicked her with such fury that she too fell to the ground stunned.

"Tall man," said Peredur, "show me which man is Arthur!"

"Be quiet!" commanded Kai. "Follow the knight who has just left, take the goblet from him and overthrow him! If you can return with his horse and arms you shall receive the order of knighthood."

"This I will do," and Peredur turned his horse and left the Court.

When he came to the meadow, the knight, who was riding proudly up and down, called to ask if anyone was coming from the Court of Arthur to encounter him.

"The tall man that was there bade me come and overthrow you," said Peredur.

"Silence!" the knight roared. "Go back and tell Arthur that unless he sends someone to fight with me soon I shall wait no longer."

"Whether you will or not," said Peredur, "it is I that will take the goblet from you and also your horse and arms."

At this the knight rushed upon him and struck him a violent blow with the shaft of his spear.

"Ha, my lad," jeered Peredur, "my mother's servants did not play with me so roughly, so I will give you answer in your own manner," and he struck the knight with his sharp pointed fork, hit him in the eye and pierced his head so that the knight fell down dead.

Meanwhile at the Court Owain was asking Kai why he had sent that madman after the knight. "For he is bound to be either killed or overthrown and, as he will be thought to be a member of the Court, he will bring disgrace on the King and on us all," and he hurried away to find out what had happened.

When he reached the meadow he was astonished to see Peredur dragging the dead knight along the ground. "For I cannot get the iron coat off him," explained Peredur.

Owain helped him to unclasp the armour and, congratulating Peredur on his victory, told him to take the horse and armour and return with him to the Court, and Arthur would give him the order of knighthood which he so richly deserved.

"That I will not do," answered Peredur. "But I beg that you will take the goblet to Gwenhwyvar, and tell Arthur that wherever I go I will be his vassal and will do him whatever service I can. And tell him that I will not come to his Court until I have met the tall man and avenged the injury that he did to the dwarfs."

So Owain went back to the Court and Peredur rode away on his new horse and wearing his new armour.

Peredur Avenges the Dwarfs

ONCE more Peredur set out on his travels, and before long he met a knight who asked whence he came, and, learning that Peredur came from Arthur's Court, cried out: "I have always been Arthur's enemy, and every man of his that I have met I have as surely killed," and rushed upon him in battle. Before long Peredur brought him to the ground, and the knight begged for mercy.

"Mercy you shall have," said Peredur, "on condition that you will go to Arthur's Court and tell the King that it was I that overthrew you and in his name. And tell him that I will never return to his Court until I have avenged the dwarfs for their insult."

This the knight promised to do, and Peredur rode on his way.

Less than a week later he met sixteen knights, and doing battle with them overthrew each one, then sent them back to Arthur with the same message as before, and rode on his way.

After some time he came to a lake on the edge of a wood, and beyond it was a fine castle. Beside the lake sat a white-haired man watching his servants fish. When he saw Peredur approaching he rose and went back to the castle, and there, sitting on a cushion before a blazing fire, he made Peredur welcome. Then he asked his guest to join him by the fire so that they could talk, and invited him to dinner, which soon followed.

After the meal was over, the old man asked Peredur if he could fight with a sword.

"If I were taught I expect I could," answered Peredur.

Then the old man called his two sons, one of which had yellow hair and the other auburn, and told them to fight together with cudgel and shield: "For whoever can handle these arms well can fight with a sword." As they fought he enquired of Peredur which he considered the better fighter, and Peredur answered that he thought the fair-haired boy could win if he wished.

"Then take the cudgel and sword from the other one," said the old man, "and see what you can do."

So Peredur took the arms, and in a moment he had struck the yellow-haired youth such a blow as to wound him severely.

This pleased the old man. "Come now and sit down," he said, "for you will be the best sword-fighter in the land. You shall stay here with me for a little while, for I am your uncle, and I will teach you the customs of the different countries and the noble bearing and manners that will raise you to the rank of knighthood. And here is my advice—if you see anything you do not understand, do not ask the meaning of it."

So that night Peredur slept in his uncle's castle, and the next morning he took his leave and rode off again.

Later that day, passing through a wood, he came to a large castle on the far side of a meadow. Finding the gate open, he rode into the hall, where sat a stately, white-haired man surrounded by many pages. Again Peredur was made welcome, and he sat by the old man when they dined. As soon as the meal was over, his host asked him if he could fight with a sword.

"If I should be taught I think I could," replied Peredur.

"Take this sword," said the old man, "and strike that staple," and he pointed to a huge iron staple for tethering horses which stood on the floor of the hall.

So Peredur took the sword and gave the staple a mighty blow which cut it in half and also broke the sword into two parts.

"Place the parts together," commanded the old man. This Peredur did, and they instantly joined as though the sword had never been broken, and the same happened with the staple. Then he struck the staple again, and again all was as before; but after the third time when he tried to place the broken pieces together he could not make them join up.

"My blessing be upon you," cried the old man, "for you fight better with the sword than anyone in the kingdom. You have now reached two-thirds of your strength, and when you have gained your full power, none will be able to stand up to you. You must know that I am your uncle, brother of the man you stayed with last night."

While Peredur was talking with his uncle, two youths walked through the hall carrying a very large spear from the point of which three streams of blood flowed to the ground. When they that were in the hall saw this, they began with loud cries to lament that which they saw; but the old man took no notice and went on talking to Peredur. Next two maidens followed the youths, carrying between them a large salver on which a man's head lay in a pool of blood. At this the wailing broke out again, louder than before; but remembering the advice he had been given, Peredur took no notice of what was going on and did not ask what it meant.

That night he spent at the castle, and next morning rode away. After some time he heard a woman's cry coming from deep in a wood which he was passing. He hurried towards the sound, and saw a beautiful woman with auburn hair with a corpse by her side which she was trying to lift onto a horse; but each time it fell off, which made her cry bitterly.

When Peredur asked what her trouble was, she answered:"Oh accursed Peredur, little pity have you ever had for my misfortunes!"

"Why am I accursed?" asked Peredur.

"Because you were the cause of your mother's death. When you rode away from home against her wishes she was so sorrowful that she died, and that is why you are accursed. And the two dwarfs that you saw at Arthur's Court were the dwarfs of your father and mother, and I am your foster-sister. This was my husband; but he was killed by the knight that lives in the glade in the wood. Keep away from him or he will kill you too!"

"You blame me unjustly," said Peredur. "Had I not left home when I did, I should not be able to avenge you by defeating this knight. Even now, so long did I stay at home, I shall find it difficult to vanquish him as I have had so little practice of fighting. But stop your tears, for they will do no good. I will bury your husband's body, then go in search of the knight that killed him."

So Peredur buried the body, and together they set out to follow the knight, whom they found riding proudly along the glade. The knight called out to ask Peredur whence he came and who he was.

"I come from the Court of King Arthur," replied Peredur.

When the knight heard this he attacked Peredur fiercely, but was immediately overthrown and begged for mercy.

"I will give you mercy," said Peredur, "on two conditions—

first that you shall marry this lady and treat her with all honour, for you have killed her wedded husband. Secondly you must go to Arthur's Court and tell him that it was I who defeated you for his honour and in his service. And tell him also that I will never return to his Court until I have taken vengeance of the tall man for the way he treated the two dwarfs."

These things the knight agreed to do, and providing the lady with horse and raiment suitable for his honoured wife, he took her with him to King Arthur's Court.

When the King received Peredur's message he was very angry with Kai for causing such a valiant man as Peredur to leave the Court. "I will search the Island of Britain till I find him," said Arthur, "and then he and Kai shall settle their dispute in an honourable manner."

Meanwhile Peredur continued on his travels until he came to a wood overgrown with weeds, at the end of which was a huge castle with many towers. Up to this he rode and struck the gate with his lance. As he did so a youth with auburn hair called out to him from the battlements to know whether he should open the gate or whether he should announce Peredur's arrival.

"Say that I am here," said Peredur, "and if I am invited I will come in."

Soon the youth returned and flung open the gate, and Peredur went into the hall. There he found eighteen youths just like the first, all slim, with red hair and of the same age, who greeted him with great courtesy. As they sat down five maidens came into the the hall, and Peredur thought that never had he seen any maid so beautiful as the chief of these. She was dressed in the tattered rags of what had once been a handsome white satin dress. Her skin was whiter than the bloom of crystal, her hair and eyebrows blacker than jet, and her cheeks glowed with the brightest red. She made him very welcome, put her arms round his neck and asked him to sit beside her. Soon two nuns came in, one carrying a flask of wine while the other brought six loaves of white bread.

These they gave to the maiden, telling her that they had less food than this left to feed the whole Convent.

As soon as the nuns left, the party proceeded to dine off the food that they had brought. When Peredur saw that the maiden wished to give him a larger helping than anyone else, he said: "My sister, I will take no more than my fair share of the meal," and in spite of her protests he divided the food equally among those who dined.

After dinner, when Peredur had gone to bed, the youths came to the chief maiden and said: "We have advice for you. You must go up to this knight's bedchamber and offer to become his wife."

"Before he has wooed me?" she said. "That indeed I cannot do."

"Unless you do," they told her, "we will leave you here alone at the mercy of your enemies."

This so alarmed the maiden that she agreed to do as they wished, and, shedding tears of shame, she went up to Peredur's room. The opening of his door woke Peredur, and he cried: "Tell me, sister, why do you weep?"

"I will tell you," she said. "My father owned all these lands and this palace, and held the best earldom in the country. Then the son of another earl wished to marry me, but I did not like him and my father would not force me to wed any man I did not care for. I was his only child, and on his death the lands came to me. Again my suitor tried to force me to marry him, and when I would not he made war upon me and conquered all my possessions except this one house, which was saved through the valour of my foster-brothers, whom you met at dinner, and can never be taken as long as we have food and drink. But we have none left except that which the nuns can give us, and now their supplies also have run out; so tomorrow the Earl will attack us with all his force, and if I fall into his hands dreadful will be my fate. Therefore I have come to you to throw myself upon your mercy, and beg that you will either take me away or defend me here."

"Go, sister, and sleep," Peredur told her, "and in the morning I will see what is the best way I can help you."

Early next morning the maiden went again to Peredur to let him know that the young Earl and all his army were at the gate. "And never have I seen so many tents, nor knights challenging others to combat."

"Let my horse be made ready!" said Peredur, and he rode out into the meadow, and threw from his horse the knight who was riding there. As the evening was coming on one of the chief knights came out to do battle, and Peredur fought him until he cried out for mercy.

"Who are you?" asked Peredur.

"I am Master of the Household to the Earl."

"How many of the Countess's possessions are in your power?"

"One-third," answered the knight.

"Then give her back the third of her possessions in full and bring food and drink for a hundred men together with their horses and arms to her court tonight, and you shall be her captive."

This the knight did for fear of his life, and that night the maiden and her household were filled with joy, and there was food and drink in plenty.

The second day Peredur went again to the meadow and fought and vanquished many of the invaders. In the evening a stately knight came out and, being overthrown by Peredur, begged for mercy, saying that he was the Steward of the Palace.

"And how much of the maiden's possessions now belong to you?" asked Peredur, and, hearing that one-third of her lands were in the Steward's control, he demanded that it should be returned to her. "And you must give her meat and drink for two hundred men, together with horses and arms, and you will remain her captive," and again all was done as he commanded.

In the morning of the third day Peredur again rode forth, and this time he vanquished more men than on either of the previous days, and in the evening he overthrew a knight of great importance.

"Who are you?" asked Peredur, and when he heard that it was

the Earl himself, he said: "You shall restore the whole of the maiden's lands, and shall also give her your own earldom, together with food and drink for three hundred men, and horses and arms for this number, and you yourself shall remain in her power."

That night there was great rejoicing in the castle, and Peredur stayed with them for three weeks to ensure that all was restored to the maiden in good order. He told her that if ever she was in trouble or danger she was to let him know and he would do what he could to help her, and with that he bade her farewell and rode away.

After he had journeyed for some time he met again the Lady of the Glade from whom he had taken the ring when first he set out on his travels. Her horse was lean and travel-worn, and he asked her whence she came. When he heard that he was the cause of her travels he was greatly worried, and cried: "He shall repent who has treated you in this way." At that moment the Lord of the Glade rode up and Peredur called out to him to stop. "For I am the man you seek, and you deserve ill of your household for the way you have treated your wife, for she is indeed innocent."

He then attacked the Lord of the Glade and threw him from his horse. When he begged for mercy Peredur said: "Mercy you shall have if you will return to the maiden, acknowledge the

wrong you have done her and proclaim that she is innocent." The knight promised to do this, so Peredur left them and rode on his way.

Some time later Peredur came to a castle and riding towards it he struck the gate with his lance. It was opened for him by an auburn-haired youth, who invited him to come inside. In the hall he found a tall lady surrounded by many maidens. She greeted him joyfully and begged that he would dine with them; but after dinner she told him that it would be better if he left the castle before nightfall.

"Why may I not sleep here?" asked Peredur.

"The nine Sorceresses of Gloucester with their father and mother are in the castle," replied the lady, "and if we cannot escape before morning we shall all be killed. They have already laid waste my lands, and nothing remains for me except this one castle."

"If you will let me I will stay here tonight," said Peredur, "and give you what help I can."

So he slept that night at the castle, but awoke at daybreak to hear the most dreadful outcry. Leaping from his bed and seizing his sword, Peredur ran out in time to see a Sorceress overtake one of the guards. He attacked her and gave her a mighty blow so that he flattened her helmet like a dish upon her head.

"I beg for mercy, good Peredur son of Evrawc," cried the Sorceress, and when he asked her how she knew his name she answered: "By foreknowledge that it was my fate that I should suffer harm from you. I will give you a horse and arms, and you shall come with me and learn chivalry and skill in fighting."

"You shall have mercy only if you vow that never more will you do injury to the Countess and her lands," said Peredur, and when the Sorceress promised him this he went with her to the Palace of the Sorceresses, where he stayed for three weeks, at the end of which he was given a horse and arms before he rode away.

That evening, passing through a valley, he came to a hermit's cell, where he spent the night. When he went out next morning he found that it had been snowing. A wild fowl which a hawk had killed lay in the snow in front of the cell, but the sound of Peredur's horse frightened away the hawk, and a raven alighted beside the dead bird. As Peredur watched he thought to himself that the blackness of the raven, the whiteness of the snow and the red of the blood upon it were like the jet-black hair, the snow-white skin and the red cheeks of the lady he loved best, and he stood long in thought of her.

Meanwhile King Arthur, still searching the country for Peredur, happened to come into the same valley. Seeing Peredur in the distance, he said to his knights: "Do you know who is that knight with the long spear standing by the brook?"

At this a young knight rode forward to Peredur and asked him who he was; but so deep was Peredur in his thoughts of the lady he loved best that he heard nothing that was said to him. Getting no answer, the young knight grew angry and thrust at Peredur with his lance; but Peredur turned and with one blow struck him to the ground.

At this, twenty-four young knights came to him; but Peredur answered none of them and dealt with each one in turn as he had the first. Then Kai, angry at their treatment, rode up and called out roughly, demanding an answer; but Peredur smote him under the jaw with his lance so that Kai fell and broke his arm and shoulder-blade, and then Peredur rode over him twenty-one times.

When Kai's companions saw his horse returning riderless, they hurried forward to see what had happened and, finding Kai lying senseless on the ground, they thought at first that he was slain; but seeing that he was not dead they carried him quickly away that he might be attended by a skilful doctor. And all this time Peredur ceased not to ponder on the beauty of the lady he loved best.

Kai's companions carried him to Arthur's tent, and the King was grieved to see his knight so badly wounded, for he loved Kai dearly.

"But it is not right to disturb an honourable knight when he is deep in thought," said Gwalchmai, "for either he is pondering on some evil that has come to him or he is thinking of the lady he loves best. If you will allow me I will go to him and see if he has come out of his deep thought, and if so I will ask him courteously to come to you," and as Arthur approved of this he armed himself and rode off.

Gwalchmai found Peredur resting on the shaft of his spear and, speaking politely, asked if Peredur were willing to talk with him,

as he brought a message from King Arthur which the other knights had already tried to deliver.

"They came with discourtesy and attacked me while I was deep in thought," answered Peredur, and he told Gwalchmai of whom he had been thinking, and of the snow and the raven and the blood which had reminded him of her great beauty. He then asked if Kai were in Arthur's Court.

"He is indeed," said Gwalchmai. "He is the knight you fought with last, and his arm and shoulder-blade are broken from the fall which your spear gave him."

"For that I cannot be sorry," declared Peredur, "for thus I have begun to avenge the dwarf and dwarfess."

Gwalchmai was amazed that this knight should know about the dwarfs, and asked who he might be. Great was his joy when he learned that it was indeed Peredur himself, whom they had all been seeking, and a lasting friendship sprang up between them. "For wherever I have travelled I have heard of your fame and nobility," cried Peredur.

Joyfully they rode towards the encampment, and when they had taken off their armour Gwalchmai led the way towards Arthur's tent.

"Behold, lord," said Gwalchmai, "here is he whom you have sought for so long."

"Welcome to you, chieftain," Arthur greeted him. "With me you shall stay, and had I known how valiant you were, you should never have left my Court. But this was predicted by the two dwarfs whom Kai ill-treated and whom you have now avenged."

They were then joined by the Queen and her maidens, who rejoiced greatly, and Arthur did Peredur much honour and took him back to his headquarters at Caerlleon.

Peredur and the Empress

THE first night at Caerlleon, when dinner was over, Peredur walked in the city, and there he met Angharad Law Eurawc.

"How beautiful you are!" cried Peredur. "If it pleased you I could love you above all women."

"I do not love you," replied the lady, "nor will I ever do so."

"I vow that I will never speak a word to any Christian again until you come to love me above all men."

The next day he left the city and rode away along a mountain ridge from which he saw a circular valley, rocky and wooded, and deep in the wood a number of large, ungainly black houses. Dismounting, he led his horse towards the wood. Ahead of him the road ran along a rocky ledge upon which was chained a sleeping lion, and below the lion was a deep pit full of the bones of men and animals. Then Peredur drew his sword and struck the lion so that it fell into the mouth of the pit and hung there on its chain. With a second blow he broke the chain, and the lion dropped into the pit; then, leading his horse, he passed along the rocky ledge and came into the valley.

In the centre of the valley he saw a fair castle, and in the meadow beside it sat a huge grey man, larger than any man he had ever seen. Two young pages were also in the meadow, one with yellow hair and the other with auburn, and they led Peredur to the grey man, whom Peredur saluted. But the grey man said: "Disgrace to the beard of my porter!" and Peredur realized that the porter he spoke of was the lion. The grey man then took Peredur back to the castle, which was a fair and noble place with tables set with food and liquor. In the castle he found two stately women, one aged and one young, and they sat down to dine, the grey man at the head of the table with the aged woman next to him, while Peredur sat by the young maiden, who gazed sadly at him.

"Why are you so sorrowful?" asked Peredur.

"For you," answered the maiden. "The moment I saw you I loved you best of all men, and I cannot bear to think of the doom that awaits you tomorrow. Did you not see the black houses in the wood? These belong to the vassals of the grey man, who is my father, and they are all giants. Tomorrow they will rise up and kill you, for this is the Round Valley."

"Listen, fair maid!" said Peredur. "Will you arrange that my horse and arms are in the same lodging with me tonight?"

This she promised, and when night came they all retired to sleep.

Next morning, hearing the sound of many men and horses round the castle, Peredur rose and armed himself and his horse before going into the meadow.

Then the two women went to the grey man and begged that he would accept Peredur's promise never to tell of what he had seen in the Valley, and let him go free.

"That I will never do," said the grey man, so Peredur fought with the giants, and by evening he had killed a third of them without receiving a single wound himself.

As the two women watched from the battlements they saw Peredur meet the yellow-haired youth, and called out for mercy for him.

"That I cannot give," cried Peredur, and slew him and also the youth with the auburn hair.

"It would have been better if you had spared this knight," the women cried to the grey man, "for he has killed your two sons, and now you yourself cannot escape him."

In fear of his life the grey man sent the maiden to Peredur to beg his mercy and promise to yield the castle into his hands.

"I will grant your father mercy," said Peredur, "on condition that he and all his men go and do homage to Arthur, and tell the King that it was I that sent them. And you shall be baptized, and I will send word to King Arthur and beg him to bestow this valley upon your father and his heirs for all time."

They then returned to the castle, and the grey man told Peredur that ever since he had owned the valley no Christian had left it alive, and Peredur gave thanks to Heaven that he had not broken his vow to the lady he loved best that he would speak no word to any Christian.

That night they all spent at the castle. The next day the grey man and his company set out for Arthur's Court, where all happened as Peredur had promised, while Peredur himself rode away from the Round Valley.

Before long he came to a vast desert where there were no houses except one mean dwelling in which he had been told a serpent lay upon a gold ring. The serpent had done much damage and had cleared the country of men for seven miles round. Then Peredur went forward into the dwelling and attacked the serpent. Long and furious was the battle; but at last Peredur killed the serpent and took away the ring. And still he had spoken no word to any Christian, and he grew weary and ill for longing for his companions and for the lady whom he best loved, and he turned his horse to travel back to Arthur's Court.

On the way he met a company of knights from the Court led by Kai, and, though he knew them well, none of them recognized him.

"Where do you come from, chieftain?" asked Kai, and getting no answer he repeated his question twice more; then, angered at the knight's silence, Kai thrust him through the thigh with his lance. But Peredur, fearing that he should be made to speak and break his vow, went on without stopping.

"You have acted ill, Kai," cried Gwalchmai, "attacking a youth who cannot speak," and he hurried back to the Court, told Gwenhwyvar what had happened and begged her to see that the wound was properly dressed.

So Peredur returned to the Court and, speaking to nobody, fought many duels and gained much fame. He was called the Dumb Youth, for he was still unrecognized, until one day he again met Angharad Law Eurawc.

"How sad it is that you cannot speak," she said, "for if you could I should love you above all men, in fact even though you are dumb, I still love you the best."

"May Heaven reward you, my sister, for I also love you," replied Peredur, and made himself known both to her and to the Court to the joy of Gwalchmai and his other friends.

Peredur remained at the Court of King Arthur until one day, when he was out hunting, he saw a hart and set his dog on it. The dog chased the hart to a desert place and killed it. Following quickly, Peredur saw that beyond the dead hart was a dwelling-place, in the doorway of which sat two bald youths playing chess. Going in, he found three ladies of rank sitting on a bench, all dressed alike, and he went and sat beside them. As one of them was weeping, he asked her why she was sorrowful.

"I weep at the thought of seeing so fair a youth as you slain, for my father, who owns this palace, kills all who come here without his permission."

"What sort of man is your father?" asked Peredur.

"One who does violence and wrong to his neighbours and does justice to none," she answered.

At that moment the youths at the door got up and put away their chess-board, and a great tumult rang through the palace as a huge black man with one eye came in. The maidens rose to meet him and help him off with his arms, and he sat down to rest, looking thoughtfully at Peredur. After a moment he asked who the stranger was.

"Lord," said one of the maidens, "he is a fair and gentle youth, and I beg you for the sake of Heaven and your own dignity to have patience with him."

"For your sake I will grant him his life for this one night," promised the one-eyed man, and Peredur drew up to the fire and joined in the feast. As they were all talking together Peredur asked the man who it was that had put out his eye.

"It is one of my habits," said the black man, "to slay whoever asks me that question."

"Lord," cried the maiden, "he spoke but in jest and relaxed with the wine, so I beg that you will keep your promise and spare his life."

"For your sake," said her father, "I will gladly do so for this night."

But the next morning the black man put on his armour and called to Peredur to rise and suffer his fate.

"Do one of two things," cried Peredur. "If you wish to fight with me, either throw off your own armour or give me arms that we may meet fairly."

"So you think you could fight me!" jeered the black man. "Then take what arms you choose."

The maiden hurried to him with arms, and Peredur and her father fought till the black man was forced to cry for mercy.

"Only if you tell me who you are, and who put out your eye," cried Peredur.

"I lost it fighting with the Black Serpent of the Cairn," said the black man. "There is a mound which is called the Mound of Mourning, and on it is a cairn. In the cairn is a serpent, and on the tail of the serpent is a stone of great value, for whoever holds it in one hand will have as much gold as he wishes in the other. As for my name, I am called the Black Oppressor, for there is not a man near me whom I have not oppressed, and I have done justice to none."

"How far away is this Mound?" asked Peredur.

"To find it you must go first to the Palace of the Sons of the King of Tortures."

"Why do they have this name?"

"A monster who controls the waters, called the Addanc of the

Lake, slays them once every day. And when you leave the Palace you will come to the Court of the Countess of Achievements."

"What Achievements are there?" asked Peredur.

"That you will learn. There are three hundred men in her household. They sit on either side of the Countess, and it is their duty to tell every stranger who comes to the Court of the achievements of the household. When you leave there you will come to the Mound of Mourning, and round the Mound are the owners of three hundred tents who guard the serpent."

"Since you have oppressed men for so long I will see to it that you can do so no more," said Peredur, and slew the one-eyed man.

"As you have killed my father," said the maiden, "all his riches and this palace are yours, and you can choose a bride from among the lovely ladies of the Court."

"I did not come here to woo," Peredur told her. "Neither do I wish for riches," and he took leave of them and rode away towards the Palace of the Sons of the King of Tortures.

When he reached it he found that the palace was full of women, who welcomed him joyfully. While they talked a charger arrived with a saddle on it and a corpse in the saddle. Then one of the women took the dead body from the saddle and anointed it with warm water and balsam which stood near the door, and the man rose up alive and greeted Peredur gladly. Later two more corpses arrived on their horses and were treated in the same way. When Peredur asked them what was the cause of these strange happenings they told him that there was an Addanc in the cave which killed them once every day, and he stayed and feasted with them that night.

The next morning the three youths set out once more, and Peredur begged them, for the sake of the ladies they loved, to let him go with them; but they refused, saying that if he were killed there would be no one to bring him back to life. So

Peredur took his horse and followed them at a distance, and when they were out of sight he saw the fairest lady he had ever beheld sitting on a mound.

"I know where you are going," she said. "But the Addanc will kill you, and that not by courage but by craft. He lives in a cave, and in it is a stone pillar behind which he hides and sees all who go in though they cannot see him, and he slays each one with a poisoned dart. If you will promise to love me more than any other woman I will give you a stone which will cause you to see him when you go in and at the same time will make you invisible to him."

"I will indeed," cried Peredur, "for when I first saw you I loved you. But where can I find you?"

"You must look towards India," she said, and, putting the stone in his hand, she vanished.

Then Peredur came to a valley through which ran a river with meadows on either bank, and on one side of the river was a flock of black sheep and on the other a flock of white sheep. Whenever one of the white sheep bleated, a black sheep would cross over and become white, and whenever a black sheep bleated, a white sheep would cross the river and become black. Beside the river stood a tall tree, half of which was in flames from root to top, while the other half was green and covered with leaves. Near this sat a youth of royal bearing with two greyhounds beside him, and Peredur and the youth greeted each other. Three roads ran from the mound on which the youth sat, two wide and the third one narrow, and Peredur asked him where they led.

"One of them goes to my palace," said the youth, "where my wife will make you welcome. But if you stay here you will see the best greyhounds you have ever known chasing the deer from the woods to kill them by the water, and, when it is time to rest, my page will come with my horse and we will return to my palace for the night."

Peredur thanked him but said that he must not stay, and asked him where the other roads led.

"One to the town," answered the youth, "where food and drink may be bought, and the narrowest road leads to the cave of the Addanc."

So Peredur went on to the cave, taking the stone he had been given in his left hand and his lance in his right. As he went in he saw the Addanc and, piercing him through with his lance, cut off his head.

Outside the cave he found his three companions of the night before awaiting him, and to them he gave the Addanc's head. They greeted him joyfully, and offered him which ever of their three sisters he should choose in marriage, and with her half their kingdom.

"I did not come here to woo," said Peredur, "but if I wished to wed I should prefer your sister to all others."

As he rode away he heard a noise behind him, and looking back he saw a man upon a red horse wearing red armour, who rode quickly up to him and said: "Lord, I come to you with a request."

"What do you need?" asked Peredur kindly.

"That you should take me as your attendant," and when Peredur asked him who he was he answered: "I am called Etlym with the Red Sword, and I am an Earl from the East Country."

"It seems strange to me that you should wish to be the attendant of a man whose possessions are no greater than your own, but since this is what you want I will take you gladly."

So they rode forward together to the Court of the Countess of Achievements, where they were welcomed with great joy. It was explained to them that though they were placed at the foot of the table it was not for lack of respect, for whoever should overthrow the three hundred men who sat above them should sit next to the Countess, and she would love him above all men. At once Peredur overthrew the three hundred men and seated himself next to the Countess.

"I thank Heaven that I have so valiant a youth as you to sit beside me," she said, "since I cannot have the man whom I love best."

"Who is he that you love best?" asked Peredur.

"Etlym of the Red Sword is his name," she answered, "and I have never seen him."

"Etlym is my companion," said Peredur. "It was for his sake that I came to joust with your household, and he could have done so better than I if he had wished. Here he is, and I will give you to him," and with great joy the Countess welcomed Etlym and became his bride.

The next day Peredur set out alone towards the Mound of Mourning, but Etlym joined him and would not be left behind. So they travelled together till they came in sight of the Mound and the three hundred tents surrounding it.

"Go to those men," said Peredur, "and bid them come and do me homage!"

Etlym rode ahead and called out to the men: "Come and do homage to my lord!"

"Who is thy lord?"

"Peredur with the Long Lance," said Etlym.

"If it were permitted to kill a messenger, you should not go back to him alive," cried one of the men, "bringing so arrogant a message to Kings and Earls and Barons."

When he heard this Peredur sent Etlym back once more to give the men the choice of either doing him homage or facing him in battle. The men chose to fight, and that day Peredur overcame the owners of a hundred tents. The next day he vanquished the owners of a hundred more; but the third day the remaining hundred chose rather to do homage to Peredur than to be slain.

"What are you doing here?" asked Peredur, and they told him that they were guarding the serpent while he lived, so that when he died the stone would be theirs, and they could fight for it among themselves.

When Peredur told them he was going to slay the serpent, the men wished to join him; but this he would not allow as he wanted the victory to be his own, and he went to the mound and killed the serpent single-handed.

Returning to the hundred men, he told them to add up all they had spent since they had been there, and paid each man what he asked, requiring of them only that they should acknowledge themselves to be his vassals. Then, turning to Etlym, he said: "Go back to the Countess whom you love best of all women, and I will go forward on my way," and to reward him for his services he gave Etlym the stone.

"May Heaven repay you and cause you to prosper," said Etlym, and they parted.

Peredur rode on till he came to a fair valley where stood many tents of different colours and, what surprised him more, a large number of windmills and water-mills. Seeing a tall auburn-haired man in workman's dress, Peredur enquired who he was.

"I am the chief miller of all these mills," said the man, and when Peredur asked if he might lodge with him the miller agreed gladly. When he came to the house Peredur asked if the miller would lend him some money that he might buy food and drink for the household, and next he wanted to know why so vast a crowd was assembled there.

"You must have come from a great way off not to know that the Empress of Cristinobyl the Great is here," said the miller, "holding a tournament, that she may find the most valiant man alive, for riches she does not need. It was impossible to bring food for so many thousands as are here, which is why the mills have been built."

The next day Peredur armed himself and rode out to the tournament, and as he came near the finest of the tents he saw a beautiful maiden dressed in satin leaning from the window of the tent. Pulling up his horse, Peredur looked fixedly at the maiden, and he remained where he was, gazing up at her all that day, for he had begun to love her greatly. When evening came, the tournament was over for the day, and Peredur rode home to the miller's house. Again he asked if he might borrow money from the miller, which made his wife angry, but the miller let him have it. The second day passed as had the first, and again in the evening Peredur begged a loan of the miller, who gave it to him.

On the third day Peredur was standing in the same place, gazing up at the maiden's tent, when he felt a violent blow on his back from an axe. Turning he saw it was the miller, who said to him: "Do one of two things: either leave this place altogether, or go on to the tournament!"

Peredur smiled at the miller and went to the tournament, where he fought with great valiance and overthrew each man who came against him. All the men he vanquished he sent as gifts to the Empress, but their horses and arms to the miller's wife in payment for the money he had borrowed, and he remained at the tournament till none were left to come against him.

Seeing this, the Empress sent a message to ask the Knight of the Mill, as she called him, to come and visit her; but he would not go, neither would he answer when he received a second message; so with the third she sent a hundred knights to bring him whether he would or not, and these he fought with and had bound and thrown into the mill waters. Next she sent a wise man, who begged Peredur courteously for the sake of the lady of his love to come and visit the Empress. Peredur went at once, and after sitting with her a little while returned to his lodgings.

The next day Peredur visited the Empress again, and while he sat talking with her a black man came to them with a goblet of wine in his hand. Dropping on one knee before the Empress, he begged her not to give the goblet to anyone who would not fight with him.

"Lady," cried Peredur, "give the goblet to me!" which she did, and Peredur drank the wine and sent the goblet to the miller's wife.

Then came a man larger than the last and also black, with a beast's claw worked into the form of a goblet, which he presented to the Empress with the same request, and again Peredur asked that he might have it, drank the wine and sent the goblet to the miller's wife.

Last there came a third man, taller than either of the others, rough-looking and with crisp hair, and all happened as before. When night came Peredur returned to his lodgings, and the next morning he went to the meadow and fought and killed the three men of the goblets before returning to the Empress's tent.

"Good Peredur," she greeted him, "do you remember your promise to me when I gave you the stone to help you kill the Addanc?"

"Indeed I remember it," answered Peredur, and he stayed with the Empress and did not leave her for fourteen years.

The Fate of the Sorceresses of Gloucester

ONE day when Peredur had at last returned to the Court of King Arthur, he was sitting beside Gwalchmai and Owain on a velvet carpet in the Palace, when in rode a curly-haired maiden on a yellow mule. Her face and hands were as black as pitch, her teeth long and yellow as the flower of the broom, and while one eye was a piercing mottled grey the other was black as jet and sunk deep in her head, and her figure was as ugly as it was possible to be.

She greeted Arthur and all the Court except Peredur, to whom she then turned, saying angrily: "Peredur, I give you no greeting since you deserve none. Blind indeed was fate in giving you fame and fortune. When you were at the Court of the Lame King and saw the youth carrying the spear from which blood flowed and many other wonders, you never asked the meaning of these things nor why they happened. If you had done so, the King would have been restored to full health and his kingdom to peace. But, as you did not, he will have to suffer wars and all kinds of disaster." She then turned to Arthur and went on: "Lord, my land is far from here, and in its stately castle are five hundred and fifty-six knights of the order of Chivalry, each with the lady he best loves, and any man who would win fame and honour will gain it there if he deserves it. There is also a castle on a high mountain in which a maiden is held prisoner, and whoever can set her free will win the highest fame in all the world," and, without waiting for an answer, she turned and rode away.

Then up sprang Gwalchmai crying: "By my faith, I will not rest till I have proved if I can set the maiden free," and many of Arthur's knights joined him in the venture.

"And I will not rest till I know the story and the meaning of the spear that dripped blood," cried Peredur.

Then the two friends armed themselves and rode forth, but each took a different road. For long, Peredur searched the country, and though he wandered over the whole island he could hear no news of the black maiden. At last he came to an unknown land in the centre of a valley, where he saw a priest riding towards him. Peredur called out to ask a blessing of the priest.

"Wretched man," answered the priest, "you deserve no blessing, nor would it do you any good since you are wearing armour on such a day as this."

"What is today?" asked Peredur.

"It is Good Friday," answered the priest.

"Do not blame me that I did not know, for it is a year today that I left my own land," and Peredur dismounted and walked on, leading his horse. He had not gone far when he came to an unfortified castle, and when he reached the gate he was met by the same priest that he had seen before.

"The blessing of Heaven be unto you," said the priest, "for you are now travelling in a manner more fitting to the day. This night you shall stay with me." Peredur thanked him and went in; but when he was about to set out again next morning the priest said: "Today no man may travel. You shall remain with me today and tomorrow, and the day following, after which I will direct you as best I can to the place you seek."

On the fourth day Peredur again prepared to set out, but first he asked the priest how he was to reach the Castle of Wonders.

"If you go over this mountain which is before us," said the priest, "you will come to a river in a valley. Here you will find the palace in which the King always spends Easter. If you can find news of the Castle of Wonders anywhere, it will be there."

Following his directions, Peredur found the valley, and there met a number of men going to hunt, led by the King himself, whom he saluted.

"Choose, chieftain," called out the King, "whether you will join me in the chase or would perfer to go straight to my palace! I will send one of my men to take you to my daughter who will entertain you till I return from hunting. Then whatever it is you seek I will do my best to help you."

Peredur, being tired with travelling, chose to go straight to the palace, and the King sent a little yellow page to show him the way.

They arrived to find the King's daughter about to dine. She greeted Peredur joyfully and placed him beside her at the table, and what ever he said to her she laughed so loudly that all in the palace could hear her.

"Surely this man must already be your husband," said the little yellow page, "or if not you must be intending to make him so," and he hurried to the King and told him what he suspected, saying: "She will undoubtedly marry him unless you are very careful and act wisely."

"What do you advise me to do?" asked the King.

"I think it would be best if you put strong men to seize him, and then hold him until you know the truth of the matter."

This the King did, and having captured Peredur he threw him into prison. When his daughter came to him and asked why he had done this, he only told her that the knight should stay where he had been put, and should not be freed that day nor the following, nor the day after that.

She said no more to her father, but hurried to find Peredur. "Even though you are a prisoner," she said, "you shall be as well treated as the King himself, and you shall have the best entertainment that the palace can produce, and if it would please you I will come and stay here too that we may talk together."

"Indeed I cannot refuse such an offer," said Peredur, so he remained in the prison that night, and the Princess gave him all that she had promised.

The next day Peredur heard much noise and bustle in the town, and asked the Princess what was happening.

"All the King's forces have come to the town today," she said, "for there is an Earl who lives near who has two earldoms and is as powerful as a king, and today our men will fight against his."

"I beg that you will let me have a horse and arms that I may watch the battle, and I promise to come straight back to my prison."

This the Princess did, and over his armour she put a bright scarlet robe of honour, and fixed a yellow shield upon his shoulder: and Peredur went to join in the combat, and as many of the Earl's men as he met he overthrew. When night fell he returned to his prison; but when the Princess asked him how he had fared he told her nothing.

The Princess then went to her father and asked him for news of the battle, and which of his men had done best in the fray. The King said he did not know the name of the man who had distinguished himself most, but that he had worn a scarlet robe of honour over his armour and a yellow shield on his shoulder. The Princess said nothing, but she smiled and returned to Peredur, and did him great honour.

For three days Peredur went out by day and fought with great valour, killing many of the Earl's men and returning to his prison at night, and the fourth day he slew the Earl himself. The Princess then went again to her father and asked for news of the fighting.

"I have good tidings for you," said the King. "The Earl is dead, and I am now the owner of his two earldoms."

"Who killed the Earl?"

"That I do not know," answered the King, "but it was the knight with the scarlet robe and the yellow shield on his shoulder."

When the Princess told her father that this was the man whom he had imprisoned he was greatly surprised and hurried to Peredur to thank him and offer him a suitable reward. "I will give you my daughter in marriage," he said, "and half my kingdom with her, and also the two earldoms."

"I truly thank you," said Peredur, "but I did not come here to

woo, but to seek news of the Castle of Wonders and how I may reach it."

"This is indeed a dangerous wish," said the Princess, "but I will tell you the way, and you shall have a guide through my father's lands and enough food to last you the journey, for you are the man whom I love best. On leaving this country you must go over the mountain you will see before you, and on the other side you will find a lake in the middle of which there is a castle. That is the Castle of Wonders, and we know nothing of what those wonders are."

Following her directions, Peredur came at last to the Castle of Wonders. The gate stood wide so he went in and entered the hall in which he found a chess-board, and the chess-men were playing against each other by themselves. Peredur stood and watched, backing one side to win; but the other side were the victors, and they started to shout and cheer as if they had been living men, which made Peredur so angry that, taking the men in his lap, he threw the chess-board into the lake. Hardly had he done so when the black maiden who had visited King Arthur's Court came into the hall.

"I do not give you welcome," she said. "You would rather do evil than good, for you have thrown away the Empress's chess-board, which she would not have lost for all her empire. You must get it back for her, and the only way to do this is to go to the Castle of Ysbidinongyl where a black man lives who lays waste all her lands. If you can kill him you will get the chess-board back; but if you go there you will not return alive."

"Will you tell me the way to this Castle?" asked Peredur. This she did, and he fought with the black man and overthrew him, and the black man begged for mercy.

"Mercy I will give you," said Peredur, "on condition that you make the chess-board return to the place where it stood when I went into the hall."

The black man promised that this should be done, and Peredur returned to the Castle of Wonders. But there he was greeted no better than before, and the black maiden abused him strongly because he had left the black man alive.

"I granted him his life," said Peredur, "so that he might have the chess-board restored to its former place."

"The chess-board is not there," she replied. "Go back therefore and slay him!"

So Peredur returned, killed the black man and came again to the Castle, and begged the maiden that she would now take him to the Empress.

"You shall not see her," was the answer, "unless you can kill the monster that is in yonder forest. It is a stag that is as swift as the swiftest bird, with one horn on his forehead as long as the shaft of a spear and sharper than anything known. He destroys the branches of the best trees and kills every animal he meets. And what is worse, he comes each night and drinks up the fish-pond, leaving the fishes dry, so that they die before morning when the pond can be filled up again."

"Maiden," said Peredur, "will you come and show me the animal?"

"That I will not, for he has let no one enter the wood for over a year. But the Empress has a little dog who will rouse the stag and drive him towards you, and then the stag will attack you."

So it was arranged, and the little dog found the stag and chased him out of the wood. The stag rushed to attack Peredur, but he stood back and let it pass, and as the stag rushed by he cut off its head with a sword.

While he stood looking down at the stag's head on which was a gold collar, a lady on horseback came towards him. She called the little dog to her and gathered him up in the fold of her cloak, then stayed looking down at the dead stag.

"Oh chieftain," she cried out, "you have indeed behaved in a discourteous way, killing the fairest jewel in all my lands!"

"I was begged to do so," answered Peredur. "Is there any way in which I can make amends and gain your friendship?"

"There is," she said. "If you go up that mountain which is before us you will find a grove with a stone slab called a Cromlech. If you will stand there and challenge a man three times to fight, then you shall become my friend."

Peredur left her and went up the mountain, and when he reached the grove and called out his challenge a black man came out from under the Cromlech mounted upon a bony horse, and both he and the horse were dressed in a huge coat of rusty armour.

They at once began to fight, but each time Peredur threw the black man to the ground he jumped again into his saddle. Then Peredur dismounted and drew his sword, upon which the black man seized the bridle of Peredur's horse and disappeared, taking both horses with him.

Left alone, Peredur walked on round the mountain, and on the other side he saw a castle in a valley with a river running by it. He went on towards the castle, and when he reached it the door was standing open and he went into the hall. There he found a lame grey-haired man sitting with Gwalchmai beside him, and he saw Gwalchmai's horse in a stall, and next to it stood his own that the black man had taken. He sat down beside the grey-headed man, who greeted him with joy, as did Gwalchmai. As soon as he was seated a yellow-haired youth came in, went down on one knee before Peredur and begged for his friendship.

"Lord," said the youth, "it was I that came to Arthur's Court disguised as the black maiden, and again when you threw down the chess-board and killed the black man of Ysbidinonygl, and when you killed the stag and fought the black man at the Crom-lech. And I came with the bloody head on a salver at your uncle's castle, and with the lance that streamed blood. The head was your cousin's, and he was killed by the Sorceress of Gloucester, who also lamed your uncle. I am your cousin, and it is foretold that you will avenge these things."

Then Peredur and Gwalchmai took counsel together, and decided to send word to Arthur, begging him to come with his knights to fight the Sorceresses.

When Arthur arrived, a great battle began, and a Sorceress killed one of Arthur's men before Peredur's face and would not spare him though Peredur cried out to her to stop. And a second time this happened, and a third; then Peredur drew his sword and struck a great blow at the Sorceress's head, splitting her helmet in two. At this she cried out to the other Sorceresses to flee, for this was Peredur, the man who had learned Chivalry with them, and by whom it was foretold that they would be undone. Then Arthur and his men set upon the Sorceresses and killed them every one, and this was the end of the Sorceresses of Gloucester.

HOW TO PRONOUNCE THE NAMES
AND MORE ABOUT THEM

(Note: In Welsh the accent comes on the last syllable but one.

"ll" is a sound peculiar to the Welsh, and the nearest we can get to it in writing is "thl".

"ch" at the end of a word should be pronounced as in the Scottish "loch".)

PRINCE PWYLL OF DYVED (*pages* 13–18)

DYVED (Dove-aid)

Probably the county of Pembroke, including also parts of Cardigan and Carmarthen.

PWYLL (Pooylth)

Meaning "Prudence".

NARBERTH (pronounced as spelt)

In Pembrokeshire.

ARAWN (Arown—to rhyme with "crown")

ANNWYVN (Anoovn)

The World Under the Earth, or Hades.

HAVGAN (Háv-gan)

PRINCE PWYLL'S BRIDE (*pages* 19–25)

RHIANNON (Reeánnon)

Meaning "a maiden". She was famous for her birds, whose notes were so sweet that warriors remained spell-bound for eighty years together listening to them.

HEVEYDD HÊN (Heváyeeth Hain)

Meaning Heveydd the Old.

GWAWL (Gwowl—to rhyme with "growl").

Meaning "Dawn".

PRINCE PWYLL'S SON (*pages 26–32*)

TEIRNYON (Tyre-neon)
PRYDERI (Prídáiry)
Meaning "Anxiety".
PENDARAN DYVED (Pen-dárran)
Chief of one of the principal Welsh tribes.

BRANWEN THE DAUGHTER OF LLYR (*pages 35–40*)

BENDIGEID VRAN (Bendigeyed Vran)
"Bendigeid" means "the blessed". He introduced Christianity
into the island.
LLYR (Lleer)
HARLECH (pronounced as spelt)
In Merionethshire. The remains of a fine castle can still be
seen.
MANAWYDDAN (Manowéethan)
NISSYEN (Níss-yen)
EVNISSYEN (Evníss-yen)
MATHOLWCH (Mathólooch—"ch" as in "loch")
BRANWEN (pronounced as spelt)
Or Bronwen. Meaning "the white bosomed".
ABERFFRAW (Abbeefrow—to rhyme with "brow")
A royal Welsh Court of old—today a small village in
Anglesey.
GWERN (Gwairn)

BRANWEN IN IRELAND (*pages 41–47*)

CARADAWC (pronounced as spelt)
In Latin the name is Caractus. He was one of the brave
princes who could never be overcome.
GWALES (Gwalais)
In Pembrokeshire.
ALAW (Allo)
Meaning "a melody". A river in Anglesey.

CASWALLAWN (Caswallown—to rhyme with "gown")
HEILYN (High-lin)

MANAWYDDAN THE SON OF LLYR (*pages* 48–59)

BELI (Bélly)
KICVA (Kick-va)
LLOEGYR (Lloiger)
  Welsh name for England.
LLWYD (Llooid)
  The same name as the modern Lloyd.

LLUDD AND LLEVELYS (*pages* 63–68)

LLUDD (Lleeth)
NYNYAW (Ninnyow)
LLEVELYS (Llevelys—to rhyme with "Ellis")

KILHWCH AND OLWEN (*pages* 71–76)

KILHWCH (Kilooch)
  Meaning a swine's burrow, in which as a babe he was found.
KILYDD (Kilith)
DOGED (pronounced as spelt)
  A Welsh saint, founder of the church of Llanddogged in
  Denbighshire.
OLWEN (Ol-wen)
  Meaning "the white trail", for wherever she walked a trail of
  white flowers sprang up.
YSPADDADEN PENKAWR (Uspathádden Penkowr)
  "Penkawr" meaning "the Giant Chief".
KAI (Ky—to rhyme with "cry")
  Sir Kay of English legend.
BEDWYR (Bed-weer)
  Sir Bedivere of English legend.
KYNDDELIG (Kinthelig)
  Meaning "the guide".

GWRHYR (Goorheer)
    Meaning "the tall man".
GWALCHMAI (Gwalck-mie—last syllable to rhyme with "tie")
    Sir Gawain of English legend.
MENW (Mennoo)
CUSTENNIN (pronounced as spelt)
    "Constantine" in English.

THE WINNING OF OLWEN (pages 77–85)

AMAETHON (Amiethon—to rhyme with "python")
    Meaning "husbandman".
GWRNACH (Goornach)
GOREU (Gorrie)
    Meaning "the best". He was so named by his companions
    because he was the only one of them who was able to
    penetrate the giant's castle in company with Bedwyr.
MABON the son of MODRON (both names pronounced as spelt)
EIDOEL (Eye-doll)
GLIVI (pronounced as spelt)
CILGWRI (Kilgoorie)
    In Flintshire.
REDYNVRE (Redinvray)
    Meaning "fern hill".
CWM CAWLWYD (Coombe Kaul-weed)
    The valley of Cawlwyd.
GWERN ABWY (pronounced as spelt)
LLYN LLYW (Llyn Lleew)
    Meaning "Lake Llyw".

THE LADY OF THE FOUNTAIN (pages 87–101)

CAERLLEON (Kirellayon—to rhyme with "crayon")
    Meaning "The Fort of the Legion".
KYNON (pronounced as spelt)

GWENHWYVAR (Gwen-hoo-yvar).
  Queen Guinevere of English Legend
LUNED (Linnedt)
  The English "Lynette".

OWAIN AND THE LION (*pages* 102–109)

URIEN (Yewrien)
  Prince of Cumberland.

PEREDUR THE SON OF EVRAWC (*pages* 110–116)

EVRAWC (Evrowk)
  Earl of York.
PEREDUR (pronounced as spelt)
  Sir Percival of English legend.
GENEIR GWYSTYL (Genire Gwistle—both "g"s hard)

PEREDUR AND THE EMPRESS (*pages* 130–142)

ANGHARAD LAW EURAWC (Angharad Low—to rhyme with "now"
  —Eyerowk)
ADDANC (Athank)
  Meaning a fabulous monster.
ETLYM (Etlim)
CHRISTINOBYL (pronounced as spelt)

THE FATE OF THE SORCERESSES OF GLOUCESTER
(*pages* 143–152)

YSBIDINONGYL (Usbidinongle)